TOO BIG TO RESIST . . .

TOO GOOD TO BEAT . . .

TOO STUBBORN TO DIE . . .

THE MULESKINNER

A novel that thunders, roars and ricochets through the violent history of the desert country . . .

A towering new story by the author of
THE APPALOOSA

"One of the finest westerns we've read in a long time . . ."

Tombstone Epitaph

the muleskinner

robert macleod

a fawcett gold medal book
fawcett publications, inc., greenwich, conn.

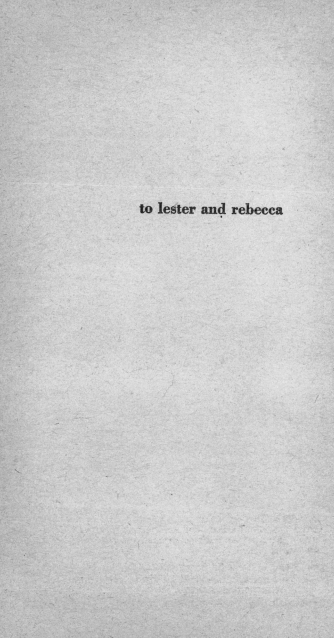

to lester and rebecca

chapter one

Ehrenberg, simmering on the east bank of the Colorado River, lay four sweating days and eighty-five miles behind, past Cullings Well and Desert Well and Tyson's Well. With Jake Harris' shaking help, Ox Davis had filled the water barrels at Cullings Well. They would dry-camp tonight and make Point Mountain tomorrow. Ox swore and jerked the line twice, and before he could holler "Gee," his smart leaders turned and the twenty mules rolled the wagons partly off the road.

Ox lowered his six-feet-three and two-hundred-thirty pounds down from Lilly's saddle and stretched, and hollered for Jake to make a fire. Sick and shaking from the booze, Jake climbed down from the trail wagon. Ox unharnessed the team and hobbled the two bunch-quitters, and Jake helped him get the feed box down, and the mules crowded around. Ox left the spreaders and the harnesses—bridles, collars, and bellybands—spaced out along the road either side of the chain, ready for easy hooking-up in the morning. There was plenty of room for traffic to get around the harnesses of the near side mules, even though they were partly on the road.

Jake had his fire going, and Ox was burning his mouth on the first cup of coffee. The sun was setting, and the desert sky looked like the inside of that abalone shell he had seen in the Cabinet Chop House in Prescott. The sand still radiated heat, and that wonderful smell of creosote bush filled the air like spice. Peace lay like a benediction on the limitless desert.

Suddenly, the mules flung their heads up and pointed their ears up the road.

The stagecoach was a dot, way ahead, dragging a banner of dust. Jake went on cooking supper, but Ox walked out to

watch the coach go by. As it approached, the shotgun messenger waved. The driver would be red-headed, green-eyed
Lew Barnes, driving his return trip from Prescott to Ehrenberg, playing his six ribbons like the strings of a guitar. Ox
had seen Lew around Ehrenberg, and thought he liked him in
spite of his arrogance, natural to all stage drivers.

The coach rattled up with the six half-broke horses in a
sweating gallop. Lew didn't even look sideways, just swung
his team so he wouldn't ram the freight wagons, and ran his
nigh horses and the left wheels right over Ox's harness. He'd
have gone right on, too, but his nigh leader stumbled over a
mule collar and the coach skidded and bounced across three
spreaders, and the left rear wheel caved in.

Ox threw his cup down and ran toward the coach. Lew
Barnes jumped down and came boiling around the rear boot,
swearing like a mule skinner and hollering did Ox think he
owned the goddamn road.

He charged and hit Ox—one, two—right on the whiskers.
He was six feet of tough muscle, and he threw his fists like
rocks.

Ox blinked and grabbed him above the elbows, picked him
off the ground and slammed him against the door of the
coach. He held him there with his feet kicking air.

Lew yelled in Ox's face, "This is a public road, you
mule-loving bastard! You leave your goddamn gear all over a
public road, I'll cut it to ribbons every time!"

He tried to grab his Colt, but couldn't reach it with Ox
gripping his arms. Ox pulled him close and banged him back
against the coach so hard Lew's teeth clicked together.

Lew snarled, "Goddamn mule skinner! Goddamn mule-
headed . . . !"

Ox slammed him against the coach again. Lew's feet
hadn't touched the ground since Ox grabbed him. Ox said,
"You had plenty of room! You didn't have to run over my
gear!"

Above him, there was a double click, and a man said, "Let
him down, you son of a bitch! I'll blow your head off!"

Ox looked up. The shotgun messenger had a sawed-off
Remington, and Ox was looking right up both ten-gauge
barrels.

Over at the freight wagons, Jake Harris yelled, "Mister, let
the hammers down an' throw it away!"

The messenger didn't waste time. When he dropped the

shotgun into the road, Ox looked over at his lead wagon.
Jake had Ox's .50-caliber Sharps leveled over the endgate and
centered on the messenger. He shifted the muzzle about three
inches, and hollered, "You, too, mister! Get rid of it!"

Then Ox saw the passenger with his head stuck out the
window. He could only be a hardrock miner. His eyes bugged
out over a tangle of tobacco-stained beard. He had a Colt in
his hand, braced on the window sill.

"Throw it away!" Jake ordered.

The miner said, "Y-yessir!" and tossed the gun out.

"Ox! Move back!" Jake yelled, and Ox moved back, dragging Lew Barnes with him.

"Everybody out where I can see you!" Jake said.

The messenger climbed down, and the miner came out on
the road.

Ox grabbed Lew's holstered gun with his right hand and
Lew's shoulder with his left, and gave one great wrench. Lew
yelled. His back bent and his belly poked out, and it looked
as if he were going to come apart. The belt buckle twisted,
the tongue came out of the hole, and gun belt and all came
free in Ox's hand. He wadded the gun and belt together and
threw them forty yards out onto the sand.

He said, "Talk about who owns the roads, you goddamn
stage drivers think you got the whole of Arizona Territory
staked out and registered."

Lew was rubbing his back where the belt had dug into
him. "You double-size son of a bitch," he said, "I'll—"

Ox reached for him, and he dodged and backed hastily. Ox
said, "You'd've gone right on, and had a good laugh telling it
all over Ehrenberg, huh? Only you got too smart and
smashed a wheel. How long you think it'll take you to get to
Ehrenberg now?"

He started to walk along the piles of harnesses to see what
the damage was. He was two steps past the shotgun messenger when he stopped, turned, put his fists on his hips, and
looked at the man. The messenger met his stare belligerently.
Ox took one long stride and slapped him across the ear. The
man's knees buckled and he staggered back four wavering
steps and dropped onto the seat of his pants. He sat there
braced on his arms.

Ox went on and picked up a mule collar that had a long,
abraded mark, but none of the gear was damaged beyond
being scuffed up.

The messenger got up. From the wagon Jake yelled, "Get rid of the Colt!"

The man still didn't seem entirely clearheaded. Carefully, he took the Colt from his holster and laid it down.

Ox took the two handguns, the messenger's and the miner's, to Jake's fire. Only then did Jake lean the Sharps rifle, still cocked, against the grub box and go on with his cooking. While he and Ox ate, the men unharnessed the team and piled up some rocks and unhooked the "false pole" that extended forward from the wagon tongue. They used it for a pry and lifted the axle and got the broken wheel off, then stood around arguing about what to do next.

Ox had cooled down. He took his time eating, and had more coffee, then went over to them. "We can rig a drag with the false pole," he said. "Sort of a Mormon brake."

They unloaded the baggage from the rear boot and, with one of the leather straps that supported the boot, secured the front end of the false pole to the front thoroughbrace bracket. When they were ready to swing the pole under the rear axle, Ox got down on his back, put his feet under the axle, straightened his legs, and lifted the corner of the coach. Quickly they swung the pole into place and lashed it in place with another boot strap.

Lew Barnes came over to Ox looking a little sheepish. He said, "I've seen you around. Never did know your name."

"Ben Davis," Ox said. "They call me Ox."

"Well, uh . . ." Lew said. He rubbed his hand over his chin. "Uh, thanks for the help, Ox. I'd never have got that drag rigged without . . . "

Ox grinned. "That's all right," he said. "Go find your gun."

He handed the other two their guns. Jake ostentatiously picked up the cocked Sharps. Ox looked hard at the shotgun messenger. The man said, "I ain't at all sure two loads of buckshot woulda stopped you."

"You work regular out of Ehrenberg?" Ox demanded. "Because if you're a man to hold a grudge . . . "

"I see what you mean," the messenger said. "When I see you, I'll buy you a drink, that's all. Guess we had it comin'." He picked up the shotgun and climbed onto the coach.

"Take it easy on that drag, Lew," Ox advised.

"I'll baby it along," Lew said.

The passenger put his luggage in, and Lew got aboard and started the horses at a walk. Ox went back to the fire and poured a cup of coffee. He looked across at Jake. "There's a bottle in the lead wagon," he said. "Under the tarp."

"I already found it," Jake said, "when I climbed in to get the Sharps. There's somethin' operates between me an' a bottle. Some kinda gravity."

He pulled the bottle from under his shirt and they each had a drink. "My lucky day," he said. "Ain't no water trough in this camp for you t' heave me in come mornin'."

Jake had another drink. "You're too easygoin'," he said. "Man did that to me, I'd bust his back was I your size. Them stage drivers think they own the world. An' you help him rig that drag an' pat him on the back. Why'n't you kiss him?"

"Oh, Lew's all right," Ox said. "Stage drivers all have delusions of grandeur."

"For God's sake!" Jake said. "Talk English! 'D'lusions of grander'! Half the time a man can't read your smoke. You talk like a schoolteacher."

"That's what I was before the war," Ox said.

"Well, you ain't one now," Jake said. "You're a skinner. All the skinners I ever seen just grunt an' make signs."

In the morning, Jake lay in a stupor in the trail wagon. Ox fried bacon and heated up the coffee and hitched up alone. He dodged Lilly's kick and saddled her, climbed on and swore at the team, and expertly hit Sam, the night leader, on the butt with a rock from the sack on his saddlehorn. The twenty-foot wagons rolled out on the six-day grind through Point Mountain and Wickenburg and up the terrible switchback grades through Antelope Valley and Dixon and Skull Valley, to Prescott.

chapter two

The uproar in the corral woke him. Most likely Leda kicking in Swan's ribs again. They were a good pointer team, but with a name like that, no mule could have any self-respect, and that was most likely why Leda kept trying to kick Swan's ribs in.

Ehrenberg was two hundred miles of mountain grades and desert roads from Prescott—ten days with a load of lumber—and he'd better get started. He crawled out of the blankets, pulled his socks up over his longjohns, put his hat on his thick, black, too-long hair, pulled on his size 14 boots, and got out from under the wagon. Nobody was stirring yet in the teamsters' boarding house operated by the O.K. Corral—too crowded last night to offer him even a mattress on the floor.

The muddy freight yard was quiet. To the southwest, the Bradshaw range had a powdering of snow, under the stars that were fading fast now. Outside the open gates of the yard, Gurley Street was one long mud-hole. Two years ago, in 1875, Granite Creek had frozen, and Prescott had had a foot of snow. Last winter, '76, had been mostly open, and the snow hadn't got down to the town, but the rain last night had been cold for May. Ox peered under the trail wagon, where a muddle of blankets covered his swamper—dirty, bearded, skeleton-thin Jake Harris. Jake wasn't much good since the booze had got him, but he still knew how to tack on a cold shoe and not get himself kicked to death, and just when to haul on the brake of the trail wagon, and when to roll the rear wheels onto the rough-locks for a steep downgrade. Coming in from Fort Whipple last night after unloading the barley and sacked flour, Jake had dropped off at Cate's Nifty Saloon, and Ox hadn't seen him since.

Ox reached under the wagon and hauled Jake—breath you could cut with an axe, whiskers, bleary eyes and all—into the open. Jake said, "Ox! No! You ain't gonna do it! I'll catch my death! Goddamn you, Ox!"

Ox picked him up. Jake's hat fell off, and a "two-bit" bottle of whisky dropped from his hip pocket. With the old man under one arm, Ox walked to the water trough, held him upside down, and sloshed his head in the water. Considering the weather, he didn't just drop him in as usual. He straightened Jake up and set him on his feet.

Ox said, "I expect you don't want any breakfast."

Jake said, "No," and, dripping, went over to the corral. Ox wiped the mud from Jake's bottle and put it in the pocket of his own sheepskin coat.

Hi Martin was still asleep under his lead wagon, across the yard. His fourteen mules were in the corral with Ox's and half a hundred others. Jake led Ox's leaders out and kicked the gate shut. He turned them loose, and Sam and Jenny took their proper places at the head of the "Fifth Chain" which was stretched out straight in the mud. Ox walked out to Gurley Street and headed for the Cabinet Chop House.

Prescott was coming awake. Sawmill hands and brewery workers were going to their jobs. A coach was loading passengers for Wickenburg at the Wells Fargo Express office on the corner of Montezuma Street, shoulder to shoulder with the shuttered, dollar-in-advance cribs. A few late or early drunks were arguing along Whisky Row. In the hills, a stamp mill made a thumping like the beating of a heart.

Ox had eight eggs, three slices of ham, twelve hot biscuits, and four cups of coffee, on top of oatmeal. When he went back to the O.K. yard, Jake had the team harnessed and ready. The saddle was cinched on Lilly, Ox's nigh leader. She was tall and rangy and all white, the only mule that wasn't bay or chestnut.

Ox walked along the line of paired mules, examining the set of collars, the fastening of traces, seeing that the jockey stick was properly in place.

People who weren't teamsters thought it was wonderful—one man handling a hundred and fifty feet of mules and wagons with only a jerk line running from him, riding the near wheeler, through the hame rings of the near side mules, clear to the bit ring of the near leader. A steady pull on the line turned the near leader left, and with smart leaders, you didn't even have to yell "Haw." Several jerks on the line, and a shouted "Gee," signaled a right turn. The jockey stick, fastened to the collar of the near leader, stretched across to the off leader and made him follow the turns. It called for smart, well-trained mules, and Ox had them.

Of course, you had to cuss them, the whole team, whatever move they were making—turning, starting or stopping. They expected it and wouldn't work right without it. Mule skinners were the best cussers in the West, or anywhere else. You supplemented the cussing with accurately thrown stones, conveniently to hand in a sack hung from your saddle horn. Ox grinned with pride, remembering how men had stopped to watch when he swung the rig that time, making a U-turn on the seventy-five-foot street in Florence, cussing his mules, calling their names, shouting out their shameful pedigrees. The mules loved it, and the people lining the street had applauded.

Ox got his ten pounds of Sharps rifle out of the wagon and

checked the load. Since General Crook had run the Apaches onto that White River reservation over east, there wasn't much Indian trouble anymore, but there were still a few loose around Date Creek and west toward the Colorado River, mixed-up Mojave-Apaches and Hualapais that hadn't been run onto a reservation, and there were renegade Apaches, sometimes, in the Chiricahua Mountains and the Dragoons, down by the border. Ox also carried a Colt .44—one of those new center-fire handguns that had come out four years ago—where he could grab it fast.

He put the Sharps in the wagon. The mules each had at least one ear pointed back at him. Jake Harris climbed painfully into the trail wagon.

Ox mounted and pulled the rope to free the brake lever from its ratchet. He got a rock out of the sack on his saddle horn and yelled, "Sam! Jenny! Swan! Leda! Hup! Git up there!" and swore at them all. He threw the rock. It bounced off Jenny's rump.

Twenty mules leaned into the collars, eight ponderous wheels turned, and the two heavy, high-sided wagons made the turn into Gurley Street, with the mules, team by team, skipping nimble as monkeys over the chain as it swung. The four Swiss bells rang sweetly on the bows over the collars of each leader.

At the saw mill, Ox hollered "Whoa!" and set the brake. Jake groaned and climbed out.

Ox said, "I won't need you on the brake between here and Skull Valley." He dug the two-bit bottle out of his pocket and gave it to Jake. "Here. If you haven't died when we get there, I'll wake you up."

Jake managed to crawl back into the trail wagon, which would go empty, this trip. Ox warned, "If you've got another bottle tucked away, I'll break every bone in your head."

"I ain't got no other," Jake said.

When the lumber was loaded, Ox shook the team up with a burst of profanity and a crack of the blacksnake. They headed through the town and cut into Sheldon Street. There, he held back the cussing, because there was a girl on the corner with some old dude with a gray mustache and a derby hat and a fancy vest with a gold watch chain across it.

The girl looked at Ox, and he wished he'd shaved in the last five days. He wasn't bad-looking, even with his slightly broken nose. Nothing handsome, of course, but women liked his gray eyes and the tremendous size of him. She was big, with blue eyes and thick, ash-blonde hair piled high under a silly-looking hat. She had a form, too. You could see that, even under the fur coat and the long skirts. He didn't have to cuss the team at all, just hit Sam on the butt with a stone and holler, "Haw!" and pulled steady on the jerk line, and Sam and Jenny swung left and the team skipped over the chain.

The wagons rolled northwest out of Prescott through Williamson Valley and turned the north flank of Granite Mountain. Skull Valley, lying studded with huge cottonwoods along the wash, brought them to the freight and stage depot near Bowers' Ranch.

The next day, they went five miles past Dixon and camped. There was plenty of graze among the pines, and Ox hobbled the two bunch-quitters. Mules were downright silly about a white mare, and most of them would hang around Lilly.

Ox had been raised among mules on the farm back in Illinois, and had ridden a mule five miles to the one-room school he taught before he enlisted. And in the war, he had driven a six-mule supply wagon before they saw how he could shoot, and transferred him to Colonel Berdan's Sharpshooters. He knew mules' obsessions and aberrations, their ability to withstand hard going and harder treatment, their capacity for work that would kill a Clydesdale. He had had affection for many mules, and Lilly was the apple of his eye.

Lilly flung her head up and pointed down the road with her ears. She had heard the coach before it careened around the bend, rocking on its thoroughbraces. As it swept by, Ox could see the nine passengers inside, and a lucky one enjoying the dust-free upper air, up on the box between the shotgun messenger and the driver. Lew Barnes, driving his return trip to Prescott, gave a condescending flourish of the whip he held along with that double handful of reins.

In the morning the harnessing in five a.m. darkness required only the customary profanity and a few wallops with a halter chain. They rolled on past Antelope Valley into the hairpin turns on the steep descent to the desert floor and Wickenburg.

The rear wheels of both wagons were braked and sliding, rolled up onto the short, ski-shaped, iron rough-locks. At each sharp bend of the road, the leaders hauled to the outside of the curve, with the teams jumping the chain as it pulled toward the inside. The pointers, just ahead of the wheelers, hauled the wagon tongue outward, countering its tendency to swing in toward the bank. The wagons rolled around the bend. As the chain straightened out, each team in succession jumped back across it.

Wickenburg was broiling, sprawled along the drying trickle of Hassayampa Creek. Saddled horses drooped at the racks, ranch wagons rattled along the street, and miners from the Vulture Mine kept the saloon doors flapping.

Ox got down and stretched, and went into a saloon for a drink. Jake had dropped off the trail wagon before they stopped, and had sidled into Peralta's store, bought his bottle, and hidden out. Ox spent the evening with a freighter who had helped him unharness and turn the mules into the corral.

In the morning, Ox found Jake with the shakes, behind the corral. He soused him in the water trough and harnessed up.

It was two long, sweating days—forty-five miles—through Point Mountain to Cullings Well. There they filled the water barrels and went to bed in the station.

Ox didn't stop at Mungia Well the next day, but went on five miles to a teamsters' camp. When he woke up at four a.m., Jake was again in a stupor, clutching a bottle to his chest. Ox let him sleep. He took the hobbles off the bunch-quitters and got the mules watered and fed—all jobs Jake should have helped with. He stirred the coals of last night's fire and had coffee and bacon, then harnessed the team. He figured to make the midday stop at Desert Well, then get a good start for Tyson's Well, twenty-eight miles beyond, before they camped.

He guessed he'd have to do something about Jake. He hated to fire the old man, who, in his day, had been buffalo hunter, Indian fighter, bullwhacker and top mule skinner; but some day, when some bunch of Apache renegades thought a few tons of supplies worth the try, Jake would be boozed up to a fare-thee-well, and you'd run out of luck.

In midmorning, Lew Barnes' coach rattled by, bound for Ehrenberg, with a full load of passengers. Ox's mules were in that shuffling trot, keeping time to the jingle of the bells. When they came into Desert Well, Jake hadn't yet shown his face. Ox unharnessed and put the mules in the corral, and went into the station for dinner. Another down stage pulled in, and Henry Bellah led his passengers and shotgun messenger into the dining room.

Henry said, "Howdy, Ox," and made a big fuss pulling a chair out for the girl. Her clothes were dusty, and there was a film of sweat on her face, but she was still as pretty as that morning he'd seen her in Prescott—about the prettiest girl he'd ever seen, and just the size for a moose like him. Ox stared into his plate of fried steak. He still hadn't shaved.

He gulped the rest of his dinner, left a bill on the table, and tried to tiptoe out so she wouldn't notice how raunchy he looked. She was talking to Henry Bellah and hadn't seen Ox get up. As he passed behind her, she was saying, ". . . as big as one of those mules he drives."

Henry Bellah said, "He sure is, an' just as stoopid!" and slapped his knee and guffawed. Ox glared at him, and he got red and looked down at his plate. The girl looked up at Ox.

"Oh! Oh, I'm sorry!" she said. "But you *are*, you know. I mean big, not stupid. Henry, introduce your friend."

Henry said, "That's Ox Davis."

Ox took off his hat. She was holding her hand out. "I'm Gwen Goodfield," she said. She nodded toward the man with the gray mustache, on the other side of Henry. "And this is my father. Daddy, this is Mr. Davis."

He still had on the flowered vest and the gold watch chain. "My pleasure," he said, and stuck out his hand but he didn't get up, just kept on talking to the man next to him. Ox was affronted, and gave his hand a hard squeeze.

"Jesus Christ, man!" Mr. Goodfield squawked. He shook his hand and flexed his fingers.

The cook brought a plate of steak and slammed it down in front of Miss Goodfield. Ox could feel Mr. Goodfield's outraged glare on his back as he walked out, grinning.

The hostler was backing the fresh wheel team up to the coach. Sam and Swan and Lilly had their heads over the gate of the corral, waiting for Ox. He led Sam and Jenny out, and the others followed, and he harnessed up. He was cinching the saddle on Lilly when Henry Bellah and the passengers came out. Henry had a clutch on Miss Goodfield's elbow as though she couldn't walk without help, but she shook him off and came over to Ox. Suddenly she went pink, and Ox was embarrassed, because he had just sidled up to Lilly and was warily lifting her tail to get it outside the breeching, and it looked a little indelicate. Lilly had her ears back, and took a cut at him with her left hind heel, but he was expecting it, and dodged, remembering not to cuss.

He snatched off his hat and looked down at Miss Goodfield. She said, "Ever since I came West, these jerk line teams have simply fascinated me. It must take a great deal of skill to handle them."

Those blue eyes just about paralyzed Ox's power of speech. "Well, uh, ma'am," he stuttered, "it isn't the skinner. Mules are smarter than the drivers. Will you be staying in Ehrenberg?"

Miss Goodfield said, "Yes, a few days. My father has a shipment of parts for his stamp mill coming up on the boat. He bought a mine near Prescott."

Henry came up and put that clutch on her elbow, grinning like a shark. Then he glowered at Ox and hollered at the hostler to get a goddamn hurry on, and the hostler fought the swing team out of the corral and managed to back them into place.

"Gwen," Henry said, "let's get you up on the box again before somebody else gets it. Always a breeze up there. No dust."

As Miss Goodfield turned to pass Ox's wagons, Jake stuck his red-eyed, bearded, dirty head out from under the wagon cover. He said, "Ox! My God, my head! Ox, where the hell we at?" His wavering gaze focused on Miss Goodfield. "Howdy do, ma'am," he mumbled, and reached up to tip his hat. He had the bottle in that hand, and it escaped him and smashed at her feet. Henry Bellah put his hand on Jake's face and shoved him back out of sight.

Miss Goodfield turned one pained glance on Ox, lifted her skirt, and swept indignantly around the broken bottle. Henry and the shotgun messenger gallantly helped her to mount the three footsteps to the driver's seat. The messenger climbed up on the nigh side and Henry on the off side. Mr. Goodfield and the other two passengers got in the coach.

Ox mounted Lilly. For reasons of his own, he didn't want to start until the coach had left, but in the corral the hostler was having a battle with the lead team, and it looked as if they wouldn't start for ten minutes.

Henry bellowed, "Goddamn you, Joe, get them nags hooked up! I got a Wells Fargo box full of bullion. We gotta hit Ehrenberg before the steamer goes."

Miss Goodfield said, "*Please,* Mr. Bellah!"

Bellah said, "Jeez . . . uh . . . gracious, ma'am, I apologize!"

He hastened to divert attention from his lapse: "What the hell you waitin' for, Ox?"

Ox thought, well, they're fed and watered and happy, maybe they'll go. He shouted, "Sam! Jenny! Hup there! Swan! Leda! Git up, now!" and got a rock out of the bag and hit Sam at the root of the tail. Sam flinched and laid his ears back, but none of them moved.

Ox glanced hastily at Miss Goodfield, whose frown showed her disapproval. Ox said to the mules, "All right, then! You're asking for it!"

He took the jerk line in his teeth and uncoiled the blacksnake and stood in his stirrups. He swung the long whip with both hands, a whistling swing with a snap of the wrists at the end, and the popper cracked like a pistol shot between the heads of his "six's". They squatted and leaned into the collars, but didn't go. Henry Bellah began to snicker. Mr. Goodfield and the two other passengers poked grinning faces out the windows.

"You gotta *talk* to 'em, Ox," Henry said.

Ox cracked the blacksnake again and yelled, "Git up there, you . . . you . . . !" Nineteen mules swung their heads and looked back at him. He could read the puzzlement, the expectation on each long face. Lilly's ears twitched and pointed back.

He looked at Miss Goodfield. The expectation and puzzlement were on her face, too, plus, now an encouraging smile.

Why doesn't she put her fingers in her pretty little pink ears! Ox thought hotly. She's heard mule skinners before! Those lunkheads just weren't going to start without the whole works, including the cussing that was their due!

One last, furtive glance at Miss Goodfield, sitting up there between those two grinning apes. He rose in the stirrups and swore and swung the blacksnake and peeled three square inches off the rump of the nigh "six," and swore again and cut a slice in the butt of the off "eight." Then he spouted such a string of profanity as had never yet been heard in Arizona Territory.

Twenty mules hit their collars as one, and the wagons rolled. He plunged his hand into the sack and pelted them with stones. When he took one last look back, Miss Goodfield sat rigid, her eyes staring ahead, her mouth a small, round "O" of shock and outrage.

Ox muttered, "Well, what the hell did you expect!" and swung the blacksnake until the wagons were rumbling down the road with the chain taut and the hubs rattling, the bells clamoring, and the mules digging in at a gallop. Jake was hanging onto the front gate of the lead wagon, hollering, "Ox! For chrissakes! You drunk, boy?"

Half an hour later, the coach emerged alongside out of the dust, and passed on the left. Henry and the messenger were grinning and waving, and Mr. Goodfield and the other passengers were laughing out the windows. Miss Goodfield sat on the box as grim as an Aztec idol, staring straight ahead.

chapter three

The chastened mules were again in that mile-eating trot. Ox sat hunched in the saddle. Dust devils pirouetted across the flats, threading their way among the ocotillo and dipping among the smoke trees in the washes. A wind began to rise, blowing away the dust raised by the chain and eighty hooves, substituting a horizontal flow of grit and sand swept up from the desert. Ox pulled his hat down over his eyebrows and tied his bandanna over his nose and mouth.

Sam and Jenny, up front, shied wildly and cut for the side of the road, snorting and looking to the right. The offside "four" jumped the chain, the "six's" reared straight up, the "eights" slammed into them, and there was a mess of mules across the chain and tangled-up doubletrees, and heels lashed out.

Grimly, Ox set the brake and got down. He unwound the blacksnake from his shoulder, swung it and popped it, and started down the line. He'd had enough from those jugheads today! And now, pretending to be boogered by a tumbleweed or the moving shadow of an ocotillo! He'd really take some skin this time!

He stumbled over something at the edge of the road, and looked down. The shotgun guard from Henry Bellah's coach lay there, a heap of tumbled, bloody clothing, with the wind sifting sand into his open mouth and staring eyes.

Ox shouted, "Jake!"

Jake mumbled something from inside the wagon.

"Get out here!"

Jake knew the tone of voice. He scrambled out, haggard but sober. He trotted up and looked at the shotgun messenger, and trotted back to the wagon. He brought the Sharps rifle and offered it to Ox. Ox said, "You keep it." He handed Jake the blacksnake. "Here. Straighten out the team and bring 'em along slow. I'll take a look ahead."

He wiped his Colt off with the bandanna and held it in his hand and started up the road. He heard the blacksnake cracking and the swearing as Jake untangled the mules.

The tracks of the coach wandered across the road in sweeping curves and scraped places where the wheels had skidded, then ran off the road into the beginning of a wash. Ox followed the turn where the coach had careened down the deepening wash, bouncing off rocks and scraping the bank. Back on the road, Jake yelled, "Whoa, you crossgrained hammerheaded . . . !"

The off leader had been down, dragged along in a crazy pattern of skidding wheel tracks and hoof prints. Around a bend, thirty yards from the road, the tracks of three running horses converged—two from the left and one down the bank of the draw—to where the coach stood jammed against the bank with its doors open and its window curtains flapping in the wind. The off leader was dead, still tangled in harness. The other five horses were gone. The sides of the coach were splintered with bullet holes. Ox hesitated, remembering Gwen Goodfield's blue, blue eyes and her red mouth and the sweet look of her. He was afraid to look inside. He stood there until, behind him, Jake yelled, "Here's Henry!"

Ox walked back. He'd missed Henry because the stage driver had fallen behind rocks where the coach had left the road. Henry was all shot up, too, and as dead as the guard.

Jake said, "They downed the off leader an' the coach swung 'round him like an anchor. How th' hell them other horses kep' a-goin' an' dragged him this far . . . What's in the coach?"

Ox said, "You look, Jake."

Jake studied the horse tracks around the coach. "Barefoot," he said, "an here's moccasin tracks. Three men, all wearin' moccasins."

He looked into the coach and stood there so long Ox wanted to yell. Then Jake said, "She ain't here, Ox. Feller with a fancy vest an' one other, but not her."

"There were her and her father and two others, besides Henry and the shotgun," Ox said. He could look for himself now.

Goodfield and another passenger were jumbled up together on the floor. Their pistol belts were nearly full of cartridges, but the pistols were gone. A valise and a carpetbag had been cut open. Clothing and papers were glued to the blood that pooled on the floor and spattered the cushions.

The cover of the rear boot had been slashed open. Suitcases and a mail bag lay inside, their contents strewn around. A fine alligator bag lay on the ground among lacy underdrawers and corset covers and a silk party dress, and spilled powder and a broken bottle of toilet water. Up by the front of the coach was the Wells Fargo box, open and empty, with its padlock shot off.

Jake said, "I hobbled the leaders an' set the brakes. Le's look around."

Two sets of footprints went on up the wash, broad prints of a man's boots and the marks of small slippers. Gwen and the passenger had been running desperately. She had fallen once, and he had dragged her and got her on her feet without stopping. There was a bit of torn cloth on the thorns of a mesquite, and three drops of blood on a rock.

Farther on, the tracks disappeared. Ox and Jake went along the wash and couldn't find them, so Jake climbed the bank and walked a wide circle. Ox yelled, "Miss Goodfield! Gwen Goodfield!" and listened, but there was nothing but the wind and the rustle of blowing sand.

Then Jake hollered, "Up here, Ox!"

Ox got out of the wash, and Jake waved and pointed at the tracks. "Feller's usin' his head," he said. "Watched for a place they could git outa th' wash an' not leave no sign. Walked her careful on rocks before they begin t' run again."

Somebody yelled, "Hey!"

They looked up and saw a man's head above a swell of ground. Ox recognized him—the passenger Gwen's father had been talking to at the table in the depot at Desert Well. His shirt was off, tied clumsily around his left shoulder, with a big splotch of blood on it. He had a six-gun in his right hand. He watched them walk up the rise.

Gwen sat on a rock behind a tangle of mesquite. She wasn't hurt, although her dress was torn and one slipper gone. Her hair hung in a tangle down her back and her face was streaked and dirty. She looked away, expressionless, as Ox stopped in front of her.

"You see any of them?" the man asked.

"They're gone," Jake said. "When did it happen?"

"I don't know," the man said. "Maybe an hour."

"We'll get you to town," Ox said. "Miss Goodfield, can you . . . ?"

She stared at him but didn't answer. The passenger sat down carefully and leaned on the rock where Gwen sat. He shut his eyes and skinned back his lips and drew a long breath between clenched teeth.

"I guess Ehrenberg's best," Ox said. "It's a lot farther than Tyson's Well, but there's a doctor, and folks to look after Miss Goodfield. Listen, Jake. Pull the rig off the road. Bring me Sam and Jenny and Swan and Leda and Lilly and Frank, with their harness and two doubletrees. And, you know, the jockey stick and the jerk line."

Jake started to go, but Ox said, "Just a second. Hobble those two bunch-quitters, and turn the rest loose. Can you handle it?"

"Yeah," Jake said, and started off.

"How bad are you hurt, mister?" Ox asked.

The passenger said, "I'll make it."

"Then just wait here till I come back," Ox said. He looked down at Gwen. "It's all right now, Gwen," he said. "It's all over. I'll be back in a few minutes, and we'll go to Ehrenberg."

He waited a moment, but she didn't answer.

He went to the coach and looked at the mess inside. He thought about putting the bodies in the boot, but he couldn't clean up the shambles inside, and it would set Gwen crazy to ride in there with the blood. He grabbed the leather cover of the boot and braced his foot on the wheel and wrenched the cover from its fastening. He straightened Gwen's father and the other dead man out, between the seats, and tucked the boot cover around them, and shut the doors.

He gathered the harness and dumped it to one side before he unhooked the traces from the dead horse and disconnected the false pole.

When he went back to Gwen and the passenger, the man said, "We were all inside with the curtains down because of the dust. Didn't know a thing till the shooting started. The coach made a swing and began hitting rocks and slowing down. They were still shooting, and Gwen's father got hit

before it stopped. He and Mr. Ford were trying to shoot
under the curtains. They both got it good, and I caught this
one."

"How'd you get away?" Ox asked.

"I shoved Gwen down on the floor, and when the coach
slammed against the bank and stopped, I got her out and we
ran down the draw. Nobody shot at us. One was still shooting
into the coach from the other side, and two of them rode
back up the draw for some reason."

"Henry fell off back there," Ox said. "Maybe he was still
shooting. How many was there?"

"Three that I know of. Maybe more."

"You get a good look?"

"Not very," the passenger said. "There was a lot of dust
and racket, and all I wanted was to get Gwen out of there."

Ox touched Gwen's shoulder. She looked at his hand, then
up into his face.

"Can you walk down to the coach?" he asked. "Jake's
bringing some mules there, and we'll go as soon as we hitch
up."

She frowned as though at some minor annoyance, and
looked away. Ox wanted to push the lock of hair out of her
eyes, push it back and smooth her hair down for her.

"She lost one of her slippers," the passenger said.

"Well, then, mister . . . "

"My name's Ostrander. James Ostrander."

"Well, Mr. Ostrander," Ox said, "guess I'd better carry
her."

She held her arms up to him and he got his left arm under
her knees and the other around her waist and straightened
up. Ostrander had a hard time getting up. Ox said, "You go
first, Mr. Ostrander, so I can watch you."

Ostrander made hard going of it, but they got to the
coach. Ox started to set Gwen down, but she hugged him
tighter and pushed her face into his neck, so he just held her
until he heard Jake cussing the six mules as they came down
the draw.

Jake was leading Lilly and Frank, and the other four
mules came along behind with the jerk line strung through
their bit rings. They were wall-eyed and nervous at the smell
of death.

Ox set Gwen on her feet. She stood with her hands laced
together so tight her knuckles were white. Her eyes were
open, but she wasn't seeing anything.

They had a lot of trouble with the mules balking, but finally got them hitched, and got the coach turned around.

Gwen still stood there wringing her hands and staring at nothing. He patted her shoulder and said, "Miss Goodfield ... Gwen ... "

She turned, frowning, and stared at him. Suddenly she smiled with a flash of white teeth, then her face went still and vacant again. Ostrander looked at Ox and shook his head.

"Jake," Ox said, "they might come back. Hide somewhere and just keep watch. If they come for the mules, let 'em take 'em. Don't take any risks. I'll come back as soon as I take her to Ehrenberg. Maybe someone'll come along, some freight rig or army wagon. Do something about Henry an' the shotgun messenger, will you?"

"I'll pile rocks on 'em," Jake said. "You want the rifle?"

"No, I've got the Colt, an' Ostrander's got one. Listen, Jake, you're doing fine. When I come back, I'll bring a bottle."

"You do that," Jake said. "Ox, that wasn't Injuns. Injuns wouldn't never leave the harness that way. They got use for brass buckles an' leather. They wouldn't of left them ca'-tridges in Goodfield's belt an' that other feller's, neither. Nor they wouldn't of let her an' Ostrander get away. Nosir, moccasin tracks, barefoot horses, I don't care. Mebbe somebody wants it t' look like Injuns, but it wasn't."

When Ox led Gwen to the coach, he had to place her feet one by one on the steps and put his hand under her round bottom and boost. She didn't seem to notice.

He helped Ostrander up to sit at her left. He said, "Mr. Ostrander, the mules won't make time like a team of horses, but I'm going to push 'em. It may be rough going. Can you hang onto her?"

"You push 'em," Ostrander said. "We'll be all right."

Ox got into the saddle and got a stone out of the sack. He yelled, "Hi-i-ya! Hup!" and jerked the line twice, then hol-lered, "Gee! Gee there, you lazy bastards!" and hit Sam on the butt with the stone. Sam and Jenny dug in and swung hard right, and the coach wracked its way over rocks and straightened out up the draw.

When they turned onto the road, he stopped and lit the nearside coach lamp. The other was shot to splinters. He got back into the saddle and shouted, "Sam! Jenny! Now you git! Git up there!"

For once, his mules started without the prod of profanity. Mules were so damn smart, maybe they knew. . . .

He whacked Frank with the end of the jerk line and kicked Lilly's ribs, and yelled at them. They raised the pace to a gallop.

chapter four

It was eleven o'clock when they pulled into Ehrenberg. Light fanned out on the dusty street from one saloon, and there were lights in the James M. Barney Mercantile and in J. Goldwater's, and a lantern hung over the entrance to R. E. Farington's freight yard. Paul Connolly, agent for the California and Arizona Stage Company, stood in front of the depot with a lantern. He said, "You're awful late, Henry!"

He raised the lantern and stared as Ox dismounted. "Hey!" he said. "Where's Henry? Who's that up on the box?"

Ox said, "Henry ran into some trouble. Give us a hand here, will you?" He put a foot on the hub and reached his arms up. "Come on, Miss Goodfield."

She fell into his arms and clung to him, and he could feel her shaking. He said, "Connolly, help Mr. Ostrander down, will you? He's hurt."

By the time Ostrander got down, four or five men had come from the saloon, and Lew Barnes was there and somehow had an arm around Gwen, and was saying, "Now, now, Miss! We'll take care of you." Ox relinquished her, and Lew said to a man beside him, "Go wake up Mrs. Hanson. Tell her to put on a pot of coffee. Tell her I'm bringing a young lady."

The man went trotting down the street and Lew followed, walking slowly and talking soothingly to Gwen. He still had his arm around her.

Ostrander leaned against the wheel and said, "Any doctor in town?"

Connolly spoke to another bystander. "Go get Doc Mace,

Cisco." He looked at the clumsy bandage on Ostrander. "You better go with him, mister. Can you make it?"

"Yes," Ostrander said.

Ostrander walked away quite steadily beside his guide. Connolly held the lantern up and walked around the coach. "Jesus," he said, "looks like a slaughterhouse."

Ox said, "It's worse inside. Her father's in there, and another one."

"Who hit 'em?" Connolly asked.

"I don't know," Ox said. "We found 'em after it happened."

By the time Lew Barnes came back and pushed his way through the bystanders, there were a dozen men around the coach. Arthur Ames came up with his shirttail hanging out. He was Ox's boss, superintendent of Farington's freight yard. He said, "Ox, where's the rig?"

"Back thirty miles or so," Ox said. "The coach horses were gone, an' I had to ... "

"Well, my God man ... " Arthur began, but Connolly interrupted: "Arthur, there's two dead ones in there. Only place I can think of is your warehouse. We can wrap 'em in a tarp, and tomorrow ... "

"Well, I don't know," Ames began, but Ox ignored him and turned to Lew Barnes and said, "Is she all right?"

"Mrs. Hanson put her to bed down the hall from my room," Barnes replied. "I couldn't get much out of her. What happened?"

Ox said, "What the hell you bother her for? She's in no shape to talk. Arthur, climb up. I want to get going."

Arthur Ames put his foot on the step and grabbed the side of the seat, and got down again. He looked at his hand and said, "That's blood, isn't it? I'll walk."

Ox drove to the freight yard and got down and lit two lanterns. Ames and Lew Barnes and four or five others came in as he was unhooking the team.

Ames said, "Haven't you got any sense at all? Leaving fourteen mules and two wagons with that drunk out there!"

Ox stripped the saddle off Lilly.

Ames said, "Answer me, goddamn it! You're responsible for that rig!"

The other five mules went into the corral. Ox swatted Lilly on the rump, and she wasn't too tired to take a one-legged kick at him.

Ames was sore, and had to take it out on something, but

he wasn't up to taking a poke at Ox. He snarled, "That goddamn, vicious . . . ! Why don't you take a halter chain to her?"

He kicked Lilly on the hock. She laid her ears back, and Ox grabbed Arthur just in time and pulled him back as Lilly's heels lashed out. Ox kicked her and bawled, "Git outa here!" and she trotted into the corral.

He coiled up the jerk line and got the jockey stick from the harness of the lead team. "What horses we got?" he asked.

"Horses!" Arthur yelled. "Now listen here! You get those bodies out of there! Wrap 'em in a tarp and . . . "

Ox picked up his saddle and bumped Ames out of the way with his shoulder. He said, "I told Jake I'd come right back. You take care of 'em."

Lew Barnes fell into step with him as he walked to the corral. Lew told him that a Chiricahua Apache, Juan Pedro, had jumped the White River reservation and taken fifty other renegades with him, and had been raiding ranches in the Dragoon Mountains.

"They wouldn't be around here," Ox said, "with troops at Yuma. Those Dragoons, they're three hundred miles from here."

"Well, you never know where Apaches'll show up," Lew said. "Hit and run, that's Apaches. Or it might be Hualapais from up around Date Creek. They killed a man working those old placers at La Paz, and that's only six miles out of Ehrenberg. The army never should have closed down that fort at Date Creek."

"Well, maybe," Ox said. "From the tracks and some other things, it might be Indians and it might not."

Lew stood around talking about the attack while Ox saddled a horse. He said, "We'll have to take care of her, you know, cheer her up and help her get in touch with her relatives."

Ox said, "See you tomorrow, maybe," and mounted and rode to the saloon for Jake's bottle.

He got to the wagons about five in the morning. Jake came out from behind some rocks. Nothing had happened. They had a drink, and suddenly Ox's knees felt as if they were going to cave in. He stretched out under a wagon and Jake put a blanket over him. He was asleep almost before Jake crawled under the trail wagon with the bottle.

The sun was well up when Ox awoke. He crawled out and

bawled for Jake. There was no answer. Then he heard Jake's snore from the heap of blankets. Well, he'd earned that bottle.

The mules were crowding around the empty feed box. They hadn't been watered—he'd forgotten to get the water barrel down before he left yesterday. He manhandled a half-full water barrel down from its bracket on the wagon, then walked over to the draw where the coach had stood, and gathered the scattered clothing and put it in the suitcases. He carried the luggage to the wagons. After he fed the mules, he built a fire and fried bacon.

The worst job was digging Henry Bellah and the guard out from under the rocks Jake had piled on them. He wrapped them in tarps and wrestled them into the back of the trail wagon. By then, he'd run out of sympathy for Jake. He booted him out from under the wagon and swore at him. Jake stumbled around helping him hitch the fourteen mules.

It was four in the afternoon when Ox pulled into Farington's yard. Arthur Ames was there, looking sourer than usual. When Jake crawled out, still drunk, Ames said, "You're fired. Any gear that belongs to you around here, get it and get out. I oughta kick your ass."

Jake bristled like a banty rooster. He walked up to Arthur and poked him square in the eye with his left fist, then teetered on his wobbly legs in a pugilistic stance. "You never seen the day you could do it!" he croaked.

Ames snarled a string of obscenities and swung at Jake. Ox grabbed him and spun him around. Spitting fury, Ames swung at Ox, but Ox's arms were too long. Ox shook him until his teeth rattled, and said, "Quiet down! You fired him, that's enough." He let Ames go. Ames shook his collar into place and straightened his string tie.

Jake leaned against the corral fence, blowing as though he'd run a mile. Ox was a little ashamed at being so relieved at not having to fire Jake himself.

"Where's Farington?" Ox asked.

"He isn't here," Ames said. "Whole town's at the funeral."

"Funeral! You mean Mr. Goodfield and that Mr. Ford? What was the hurry?"

"You sure run to muscle, not brains," Ames said. "You got any idea what the temperature is?" He started for the office.

"Just a minute, Arthur!" Ox went after him. "You fired Jake, but you didn't pay him."

"He'll wait. Payday's the end of the month," Arthur said, and went into the office. Ox followed him in. The manager sat down at the table and began to fiddle with some papers.

Ox said, "What about Henry Bellah and the messenger? I got 'em wrapped up in the wagons."

Ames sighed in exasperation. "Oh, God! Well, put 'em in the warehouse, like the others."

"That's the swamper's job, and the yard help. But you just fired the swamper. Well, so long, Arthur. Better get to work. Awful hot in that wagon."

Jake had gone somewhere, so Ox went to his room behind the office, where there were sleeping quarters for teamsters. He got his blue suit and clean underwear and a clean shirt and took them to the Chinaman's.

Half an hour later, when he came out of the bathroom behind the barber shop, clean and feeling light on his feet, and wearing only his longjohns, he got into the barber chair and gave himself over to the delight of the hot towels and the feather touch of the razor. The Chinaman brought the pressed suit and the ironed shirt.

He wasn't due to take a load out until tomorrow, and he figured he'd earned a drink or two before dinner.

He went into the saloon, and men crowded around with questions. Jake was at the bar, and Ox pushed his way over to him, thinking maybe Jake was running up a bill he couldn't pay. Jake was mumbling, "Goddamn fool! Barefoot horse tracks! Moccasin tracks! That's all he can think of! Stupid damn fool!"

Ox slipped a five-dollar piece into Jake's pocket. "Who?" he asked.

"Him," Jake said, and pointed with his chin, like an Indian. Ox looked, and Lew Barnes, all slicked up in a black suit and white shirt and black string tie and polished boots, grinned at him from a corner table. He must have come from the funeral. Farington was there with him, and Jim Barney from the Mercantile.

Jake shook his fist at Lew and hollered, "Wasn't Injuns, ye damn fool! Think I don't know Injuns? Think I didn't scout for Crook? What the hell you know 'bout 'Paches!"

Lew beckoned to Ox, and he shoved his way over to the table. Seemed like the whole five hundred inhabitants of Ehrenberg were in the saloon after the double funeral.

Lew Barnes said, "I'm buying. What's yours, Ox?"

"I'll have one of those cocktails, since I'm all dressed up,"

Ox said. "Lew, how's Miss Goodfield? You see her at the funeral?"

Lew said, "She hasn't got any relatives, not anybody. We all ought to sort of look after her till she knows what she wants to do."

Farington said, "We found some addresses in Ford's pocket. Sent a telegram to his relatives."

"What about Ostrander?" Ox asked.

"Doc put about eight pounds of plaster of Paris on him. Broken collarbone and a hole in his shoulderblade. He's up and around, somewhere. Tough man, that!"

"Mr. Farington," Ox said, "Arthur fired Jake."

"Jake already told the whole town, Ox. Now, listen. It sticks, this time. We just can't depend on him, can we?"

Reluctantly, Ox said, "Well, you're right. Thing that bothers me is what's going to happen to him."

Lew Barnes said, "You're well rid of the old futz!"

They all turned toward the bar. The barkeep was helping Jake into the back room. When he came back, Lew said, "Set 'em up over here, Charlie. Bring the bottle."

The barkeep brought the bottle and Lew poured a round, while the barkeep rang it up and brought change.

Lew tossed his drink down and lit a cigar. He said, "That Gwen, she's got backbone. Oh, Ox, I forgot. She wants to see you, down at Mrs. Hanson's."

Ox set his drink down untasted, and went out.

When Mrs. Hanson let him into the parlor of her rambling adobe, Gwen was there, white and exhausted. Her eyes were swollen. She got up and took his hand in both of hers. For a moment, she couldn't speak, and tears welled in her eyes. Ox wanted to pat her shoulder and tell her not to cry.

She blew her nose and said, "Mr. Davis . . . "

"Aw, it's just Ox, Miss Goodfield," he said.

"That's an awful name. I couldn't call you that!"

"Well, Ben, then," he said. "That's my real name."

"Ben, I won't even try to say . . . I mean, I don't know how I can ever . . . "

"Now, listen here, Miss Goodfield . . . "

"Gwen," she said, and squeezed his hand.

"What are your plans?" he asked.

"Oh, I haven't been able to think, yet. I don't know. I'll have to go back to Prescott, I think. There's Daddy's mine there, and . . . " She gulped and wiped her eyes.

"Well," Ox said, "I suppose you have the registration papers and things like that."

"Oh . . . " She began to sniffle again. "I . . . I don't know. He didn't trust banks much. Mr. Ames brought me his suitcase this morning, but everything is all mixed up, his clothes and papers and . . . " She was crying hard now.

Ox felt helpless and sad. She stopped crying and blew her nose and said, "I don't even know if Daddy made out a will. Maybe his lawyer in Prescott knows. Maybe he has the mine papers, if they aren't in the suitcase. And there's the machinery coming up on the steamer. That's why we came here, and that's why"—her chin trembled—"why he was carrying so much cash. That's why they robbed the coach, I guess, if they knew."

Ox said, "Might have been just a happenstance, Gwen. Henry Bellah had a Wells Fargo box full of bullion. There's ways they could have found out about that. Was he carrying a lot?"

"More than five thousand dollars in bills and gold."

"Whew!" Ox exclaimed.

"He liked to deal in cash," Gwen said. "It always worried me."

"Gwen"—Ox hesitated—"somebody said you didn't have any relatives."

"Nobody, now," Gwen said. "Not a soul in the world." She bit her lip and turned away. Ox reached his hand out, then pulled it back.

He said briskly, "Well, now, I expect you'll need some cash until they recover the money. Now . . ." He got his wallet from his pants pocket.

She said, "Oh, no! Really, I couldn't! Mr. Barnes insisted on lending me a hundred dollars, and, well, I took it."

Ox thought about that, and didn't like it. Then he thought he should be going, but kept trying to think of some excuse to stay. "When are you going to Prescott?" he asked.

"Oh, Ox . . . Ben, I mean . . . I don't know. It all happened so fast. Daddy has a . . . there's a house we rented in Prescott, and I'll have to see the lawyer, but I just want to have a little while to think."

"Will you stay in Prescott?" he asked. "Are you going to live there?"

"I just don't know yet. I liked California when I came out in '75 to join Daddy, and then we came to Arizona and, well, it's nice around Prescott, lots of nice people there, and churches and schools, but it's pretty rough. I mean the miners and soldiers, and that awful Whisky Row. I was beginning to like it, though, and then this happened."

She got up. "Well, Ben," she said, "come and see me again. I'll be here a few days. They said the steamboat got stuck on a sandbar, and they don't know when it will get here, and I have to do something about Daddy's machinery. They said there's a platoon of soldiers on it, too, coming up from Yuma to try and find those Indians. What could Indians do with Daddy's money and the gold shipment? Wouldn't they get caught if they tried to spend it?"

"Well, Gwen, I don't think soldiers or anyone could catch 'em, not right away. Maybe they'll give themselves away somehow."

She walked to the door with him. "When do you leave again?" she asked.

"I'm waiting for the steamer, too," he said. "Some machinery for the Vulture Mine and the rest of it for Prescott. Now, Gwen, if you need anything else ... I mean, I have some money saved up. You just ... " he stopped awkwardly.

She smiled then, and caught hold of his lapels. "You have to bend down," she said. "You're so big!" And before he knew what she was up to, she pulled him down and kissed him on the cheek. He stared at her with his mouth hanging open.

She said, "I don't need any more, Ben. Mr. Barnes suspected I didn't have any, that Daddy ... well, that those men took all we had ... and ... it was very thoughtful of him."

As he went out, she smiled and said, "Come and see me again."

He stalked up the street, half sore because Lew had been smarter than him, and half elated because she'd kissed him. Then he thought, she probably kissed him, too—about a hundred dollars' worth. By God, he needed a drink!

The saloon was layered with smoke and loud with teamsters and townsmen and miners. Paul Connolly, the stage agent, stood with his elbows on the bar, looking across the room at a noisy stud game—a teamster and a clerk from the steamboat office, and what looked like a couple of buffalo hunters, one of them bearded, both long-haired and greasy.

The barkeep poured Ox's whisky, and Connolly said, "How do buffalo hunters always manage to be so filthy? I can smell 'em from here!"

Ox slugged down his drink and said, "Those two are a long

way from the hunting grounds. There's no buffalo closer'n Colorado or maybe the Texas Panhandle, are there?"

"They're a fiddle-footed lot," Connolly said. "I hunted with Comstock and Billy Dixon. It's impossible to keep clean in camp, but you'd think they'd at least wash up when they get with civilized people. Probably they made a good winter hunt and sold their hides and are out to blow it."

Lew Barnes came breezing in, still wearing the black suit and white shirt. He was smoking a cigar, and his face was flushed. He looked the room over, but didn't seem to see Ox or Connolly.

Connolly said, "Well for God's sake!" and thumped his glass down on the bar and started across the room. Ox finished his drink and walked after him.

At the poker table, Barnes was saying, "You boys want another victim? I'm loaded for bear."

The teamster said, "Sure. Set in. Table stakes, five-dollar limit."

The players moved to make room, and Barnes dragged over a chair from the next table, and just then Connolly grabbed his shoulder and turned him around. He said, "Lew, what the hell's this? The team was hooked up half an hour ago, and the baggage is loaded and the passengers are waiting."

Barnes looked Connolly up and down. He looked at his cigar and put it in his mouth and took a long drag, and blew the smoke in Connolly's face. He said, "Didn't I tell you, Paul? I just quit."

"You *quit*?" Connolly said. His face flushed. "Just like that, huh? With a coach full of passengers and U.S. mail in the boot! What am I supposed to do for a driver?"

The big room was still, and everyone watching. Barnes said, "You want me to tell you where you can shove the passengers and the coach and the mail?"

Connolly hit him a good one on the mouth. It turned Barnes half around, but he caught the back of a chair and didn't go down. Connolly watched him for a few seconds, apparently thought Lew was going to just take it, and turned to go out.

"I'll drive the run myself," he said. "You've driven your last one for any C and A line."

Barnes charged him, swinging. Connolly ducked and took punches on his arms and coolly watched for his opening. Too mad and too eager, Lew wasn't doing much damage, just swinging wild. Connolly would nail him in a minute. They crashed into the poker table, and somebody across the room raised the long, rebel yell. The big teamster got up, grinning, and slung a chair aside and spat on his hands. He said, *"Well, now! Fun for everybody!"* and lowered his head and charged at the fighters.

Ox wasn't sure which man the teamster was after—he probably didn't care. As the man plunged past, Ox clubbed him on the back of the neck with his right fist, and the teamster's rush continued without pause. He plowed into the floor, face first.

Ox whirled, trying to watch everyone at once. Anyone might get excited, or catch a stray punch and start shooting. Men were crowding around. Connolly and Barnes were still swinging, with their forgotten guns bouncing on their hips. The two buffalo hunters were backed against the wall. The tall, skinny one with the beard was grinning, his long yellow teeth showing. He had a bowie knife in his right hand. Ox grabbed up a chair by its back and shoved the clerk aside and walked warily toward the buffalo hunter, with the chair swung back ready to smash him. The hunter took one cat-footed step toward Connolly, glanced swiftly around and saw Ox with the chair. He stopped and licked his lips and moved back against the wall. He put the knife away, but Ox continued to watch him, while everybody yelled and feet stamped and the barkeep yelled, "Now, now! Gentlemen! That's enough!"

The racket subsided. Ox looked around. The barkeep had a sawed-off billiard cue in his hand, and a couple of men were holding Lew Barnes. There was blood on Lew's mouth. Connolly was breathing hard. His coat collar was torn and his shirt tail was out, and one of his eyes was going to swell shut before long.

They poured water on the teamster, who still lay face down with his arms sprawled out. He rolled over and sat up. His face was scraped raw from plowing into the floor. He shook his head and began to rub the back of his neck.

Paul Connolly went out. They set up the overturned table and picked up the chips. Ox went back to the bar and had a drink. Lew sat at the poker table, glowering and fingering his swollen mouth.

The teamster struggled up and wobbled to a chair and sat down. After a while, he got up and walked to the bar, staggering only a little. He had two drinks, looked Ox over, then walked along the bar and faced him.

He said, "Guess it was you, huh?"

Ox turned his left shoulder toward him and hung his balled-up right fist down by his knee, and said, "Yeah."

"You didn't use no club or brass knuckles?"

"Uh-uh," Ox said.

"Well, then, le's have a drink."

He got pretty drunk with the teamster, and Lew Barnes joined them, and about eleven o'clock, Lew and Ox went singing down the street to Mrs. Hanson's boarding house. Before they got there, Ox said, "Sh-h-h! Shut up! Mustn't wake Gwen up!"

"Tha's righ'," Lew said. "Abs'lutely righ'!" He went tiptoe-ing with elaborate caution to the door. Ox headed for his room behind Farington's office.

chapter five

Ox awoke with a big head and a vile temper. He pulled the blanket over his head, trying to shut out the morning noises of the freight yard—a skinner cursing as he hitched up, the slamming around of barrels and crates on the loading platform. Every sound drilled into his skull like a gimlet. He swore and got into his working clothes. Shaving, he cut his chin, and swore again, knowing the damn thing would bleed for an hour. Shaving two days in a row—what had got into him! Gwen would never look at him twice and, anyway, she'd be gone in a day or two.

Six fried eggs and a stack of flapjacks at the Canton Restaurant improved his health and disposition.

When he went to the freight yard, Arthur Ames was just throwing Jake out the gate. Jake scrambled to his feet, snarling like a bearded weasel at bay. Arthur said, "God-damn drunk! You keep out of here!" He looked at Ox and said, "We're loading your lead wagon. He slept there."

Ox said, "I won't drive without a swamper. Why don't you keep him till the end of the month?"

"Not him," Arthur said. "You don't go till tomorrow. Steamer won't be in till tonight, and we'll load the machinery in the morning. We'll find you a swamper." He turned toward the office.

Ox grabbed his shoulder and turned him back. "Why the hell don't you pay him off, then?" he demanded.

Arthur tried unsuccessfully to knock Ox's grip loose. He said angrily, "Payday's the end of the month."

"You're a nasty little slug, Arthur," Ox said, and gave him a shove that made him trot to keep his feet. Arthur called him a dirty name and went into the office.

Ox gave the old man ten dollars and said, "There's that Mexican lady, Mrs. Leyva, down by the ferry landing. Get a room there. I'd let you stay here, but you'll be drunk by noon, and I can't stand you."

"You're all right, Ox," Jake said, and headed for the saloon across the street.

Ox had put on a clean shirt and the blue suit, and stuck a piece of paper on his bleeding chin. He just might meet Gwen by accident. And an hour later, he did. She was coming out of Goldwater's store with Mrs. Farington, and her arms were full of bundles.

"Hello, Ox," Mrs. Farington said. "I heard you lost your swamper. Heard you were brawling in the saloon last night, too. You and Lew Barnes."

Ox blushed, and Mrs. Farington laughed at him. "He's a good boy, Gwen," she said. "Compared to most mule skinners, that is. Best mule man we ever had."

"You're all dressed up, Ben," Gwen said. "Aren't you driving today?"

"Not till tomorrow," Ox replied. "Steamer's late with that stuff from Yuma."

Mrs. Farington said, "Why don't you carry Gwen's packages for her? That will keep you out of the saloons for a while, anyway." She took Gwen's bundles and pushed them at him, and when he had them, gave him a push to start him down the street. Gwen fell into step beside him.

He couldn't think of anything to say, and presently Gwen said, "Lew quit his job. He might go to Prescott. Might even be interested in the mine Daddy bought. He ought to get into something with a future. He's capable of much more than just driving a stagecoach."

So what's wrong with driving a coach, Ox thought. And where would Lew Barnes get that kind of money? A hundred and twenty-five a month wouldn't buy many gold mines, especially if you sat in too many stud games.

"I'll probably stay there a while," Gwen was saying, "to get things straightened out if Daddy didn't leave a will. It would be nice to have Lew there, somebody I know."

Ox burned with jealousy. "What's *he* know about mining?" he blurted. "All he's done since the war, the way I hear it, is pour leather into six horses, and drink and play poker between runs."

"Now, Ben, is that nice? His family is well-off, back in Virginia. He'll come into quite an estate some day."

"Did *he* tell you that?" Ox asked. "I never heard any such thing."

"Why, Ben! I believe you're jealous!" Gwen laughed and he felt his face get hot. But she squeezed his arm when she took her packages in front of Mrs. Hanson's house. "You'll be freighting to Prescott, and I'll see you there, too."

That had him stepping high as he walked back. The coach for Dos Palmas went by, heading for the ferry across to the California side, and Mr. Ostrander waved at him from a window. Ox waved and went into the saloon.

Lew Barnes was at a table, talking to the two buffalo hunters. He waved at Ox to come over, but Ox didn't like the long-haired, bearded, yellow-toothed hunter who had pulled that bowie last night. He took a look at the other one, shorter and fat, long-haired too, but clean-shaven, if you could call it that, with three days' stubble around his pursy red mouth. He didn't like him either, so he stayed at the end of the bar and made a shambles of the free lunch.

Jake came in. He wore clean Levi's and a clean shirt, and had even trimmed his beard. He'd had a couple of drinks, but wasn't drunk yet. He said he thought he'd go to Prescott or Florence and get a job, when Arthur Ames paid him his wages.

"That's fine!" Ox said. "I'm sorry I couldn't put in a word for you yesterday, but I . . . "

"Aw, forget it," Jake said. "I know why. Yessir, soon as Arthur pays me off, I'll go to Prescott."

Ox had his doubts, but he just said, "You do that, Jake."

In the afternoon, Ox took a walk down to the ferry landing, and saw smoke, way down the river. The sternwheel-

er would be tied up before dark. He had supper at the
Canton Restaurant and went to bed early.

When he got up, wagons were bringing the machinery up
from the steamer, and swampers and roustabouts finishing
the loading of his trail wagon. When he came back from
breakfast, his new swamper, a gangling youth, was having
trouble getting the mules out of the corral. Arthur Ames was
bawling at him, making things worse.

Ox was about to go over and run Arthur back to the office
and straighten things out, when Gwen called to him from the
gate. He walked over, his smile fading and the big leap of his
heart dying when he saw Lew Barnes hanging onto her arm.
Lew was all duded up, with a new white Stetson and new
boots.

"We were down to the steamer," Gwen said. "They'll store
Daddy's machinery until somebody buys it. We wanted to see
you before you go, to tell you good-bye. We're leaving for
Prescott tomorrow."

We! Ox thought. So that son of a bitch is . . .

"I'll be expecting you," Gwen said. "My house is the brick
one on Leroux, around the corner from Marina."

He was about to say something he'd be sorry for, when he
heard Lilly squeal. In the corral gate, Lilly was on her hind
legs, her ears flat, striking out with her forefeet. The scared
swamper was at the full length of the halter chain, jerking on
it. Arthur Ames ran to the corral fence and grabbed another
halter with its six feet of chain. He yelled, "Hold that
goddamn bitch mule! I'll peel her from ears to ass. Any
goddamn driver that can't beat sense into a mule oughta
be . . ."

He swung the chain and brought it cracking down across
Lilly's back. Ox got there at the same time. He jerked the
chain from Arthur's grasp and batted Arthur on the head
with his left hand. Arthur's head thumped on the gatepost,
and he slumped down in a heap.

Ox slapped Lilly's shoulder and yelled, "Get in there,
goddamn you!" She kicked at him and he dodged. He booted
her in the rump and she trotted back into the corral.

He turned to Arthur and yelled, "You keep your hands off
my mules!" and Arthur, with a snarl on his face and a trickle
of blood at the corner of his mouth, fumbled at his coat
pocket and pulled a nickel-plated revolver.

Ox whipped him across his gun hand with the halter chain,
and the gun went spinning as Arthur squealed with pain. Ox

plucked him off the ground, slammed him against the post, and pulled back his right fist.

Gwen screamed, *"No! No! No!"*

Ox stopped the punch just in time. Arthur hung limp in his grasp with his face white as lard.

"Ox! Don't you hit that man!" Gwen screamed. Ox let him down.

Arthur caught his balance and squealed into Ox's face, "You're fired, you son of a bitch! You're fired!"

Ox slapped him. "You shut up," he said. "Get me my money. If I stay here, I'll break your head some day."

Arthur rubbed his sore hand and snarled, "Money, hell! Try and get it!"

Ox wrapped the chain under Arthur's arms and fastened the snap hook and, while Arthur spat and kicked, boosted him off the ground and hung him up with a turn of the chain around the top of the gatepost. Ox started for the office, while Arthur cursed and twisted, trying to reach the snap hook.

Gwen stood white-faced, her eyes like blue marbles. Lew had a grin from ear to ear.

Ox banged the office door open and stamped across to the desk. He knew where Farington kept the key to the inner door of the safe. He took two weeks' pay in cash for himself, and two weeks' for Jake Harris, and went back to the desk and wrote a receipt.

When he went out, Farington, himself, had released Arthur from the chain. A couple of helpers scuttled out of Ox's way as he strode across the yard. Arthur was brushing himself off, almost blubbering, and was saying to R. E. Farington, "And then he . . ."

Ox said, "Shut up, Arthur!"

"Ox! What's wrong here?" Farington demanded. "What the hell you think you're doing?"

"Nobody lays a hand on my mules!" Ox said. " 'Specially not Lilly!"

"Your mules!" Arthur yelled.

"Those mules are the property of R. E. Farington," Farington said. "In case you forgot, that's me!"

"All right!" Ox bellowed. "But I run 'em! If anybody's gonna whale 'em with a chain, *I'll* do it! Not him, an' not you, either!"

"I'll whale that white killer!" Arthur snarled. "I'll cut her to rags!"

Ox said softly, "Arthur-r-r!" and raised his hand, and Arthur scuttled behind Farington.

"What's Lilly worth, R. E.?" Ox asked.

Suddenly, Farington grinned. "Well, I'll be damned! You and her deserve one another! Nobody else could ever handle her. Fifty dollars?"

Ox got the wad of bills out of his hip pocket and counted out fifty. "Arthur's full of poison, like a Gila monster," he said, "only he hasn't got the guts to work it off in a good saloon brawl. He'd rather take it out on a tied-up mule. He'd take it out on her for sure after I leave."

"What do you mean, leave?" Farington asked. "You quitting?"

"R. E., if I stay around, I'll break that slug's neck," Ox said. "Oh, yeah"—he held out the receipt he'd written—"I took our pay, mine and Jake's."

Farington took the receipt, and stood pinching his lower lip. Then he said, "Well, I guess it's best, Ox. If you hit Arthur like you slugged that teamster, you'd kill him. Use the back room till you're ready to go. If you want a letter to Ed Carlson down in Tucson, why . . ."

"Thanks," Ox said. "I know Ed. I freighted out of Tucson."

The helpers were loading again, and Arthur Ames picked up his pocket gun and went into the office. Gwen and Lew still stood in the gateway. Somewhat shamefaced, Ox walked over to them. He was trying to frame some sort of apology to Gwen—not that he was ashamed of his outburst, but it must have been unpleasant for her.

She said, "You ought to control that temper, really! And such language!"

Lew grinned. "Arthur's been spoiling for something like that for a long time," he said.

Gwen relented and smiled at Ox. "Anyway, I'm glad about Lilly, Ben. I saw him hit her with that chain. Do you really like mules better than people?"

Ox wanted to tell her that he liked *her* better than people— better than any other person in the world. It must have shown in his eyes, because she turned pink and looked away.

Lew said, "Well, everybody's out of a job, huh? You and me and Jake. What are you going to do?"

Ox said, "Well, go to Tucson, maybe. I'll take a freighting contract, if I can get a team and wagons on credit."

"Why don't you go with us tomorrow?" Gwen asked. "At least as far as Wickenburg."

Lew suddenly looked sour. He said, "He's got a family, now. They don't take mule passengers on the stage."

"That's right," Ox said, "I'll be ridin' that Lilly mule."

"All that way across the desert?" Gwen asked. "In the heat, and no water?"

"Oh, that isn't hard," Ox said. "The stage stops aren't far apart, and there are teamsters' camps with wood an' water in between."

"And when Lilly gives out," Lew said, grinning, "why, they just switch over and Ox carries *her*."

Ox wished Lew would go away so he could say good-bye to Gwen by herself, but he stuck to her like a cholla branch, so Ox said, "Well, good-bye, Gwen. I'll get to Prescott once in a while."

She held out her hand. "Good-bye, Ben. I won't forget you, ever."

Lew said, "So long, Benny!" He was still grinning, and Ox turned away so he wouldn't give in to the temptation to slug him.

He didn't have much to pack—some underwear and shirts and his blue suit, and his razor and shaving mug and odds and ends. It all went into one carpetbag. He went over to Goldwater's and bought two blankets and a couple of two-quart canteens and a box of .44 cartridges for his Colt.

Lilly was on her best behavior when he saddled her. He stowed some small things in the saddlebags, along with a couple of quarts of barley, and wrapped the carpetbag in the blankets, with his sheepskin coat around everything, and tied the bundle behind the cantle. He hung the canteens on the saddle horn.

Farington came out and said good-bye. Ox got his Sharps rifle, the design the makers called "Old Reliable," hung its cartridge belt around his shoulder, and was ready to go.

He knew where to find Jake. In the saloon, Jake said, "Heard you quit. Where you goin'?"

"Tucson," Ox said. He gave Jake his wages and said, "You ought to get out of Ehrenberg before you drink it all up, Jake."

"I ain't been drunk for two days now," Jake said. "Not what you could call real drunk. Well, see you some place. Take care, boy."

chapter six

Ox was in no particular hurry, and figured to do the 275 miles to Tucson in about ten days. It was the beginning of June, broiling hot and bone dry, and they started out at dawn each day, and rested at any station they might reach about noon, until the sun didn't beat straight down on their heads like a singlejack sledge.

Phoenix and Florence were busting at the seams, the sleepy old adobe towns with their tree-lined *acequías* now only the nuclei of clusters of new industries—mills, breweries, commercial establishments—and so crowded that teamsters camped on the desert for want of accommodations.

Ox found Hi Martin in the Sazerac Saloon in Florence, and learned that the murderers of Gwen's father had not yet been caught.

He bought a copy of "The Citizen" and took it to the Plaza Stable, where he had managed to get a stall for Lilly. He, himself, would sleep on the hay—there wasn't a hotel room to be had.

The headlines said, "RENEGADES STRIKE IN WHETSTONE MTS."

"On June 2, a patrol of Company I, Sixth Cavalry, Fort Bowie, found the bodies of two miners, A. F. Alford and an unidentified man, on their claim near Old Camp Crittenden. Both had been tortured. According to Captain W. Wallace, Fort Bowie commandant, the atrocity is the work of Juan Pedro, one-time sub-chief of Cochise, and his band of renegades from the White Mountain reservation. The patrol, led by Apache trackers of the Indian Police, came upon the tragedy in the course of their pursuit of the band after an attack on Henry Helm's ranch north of Camp Crittenden, in which Helms and his son Henry, Jr., 8, were killed. Captain Wallace reported that the Juan Pedro band has presumably reached Sonora. Pursuit will continue in collaboration with Mexican forces of that State."

Rolled in his blankets, Ox got to wondering if it could have been Juan Pedro's band that hit the coach up there by Desert Well. Didn't seem likely—they couldn't be in two places at once, but maybe the pressure of pursuit had driven some of them north. He had a sudden, vivid memory of Gwen's stricken face. He could almost feel her arms tighten around his neck, and the frustration of his inability to find one comforting word. Lew Barnes wouldn't have just stood there dumb, hanging onto her. Not him! Most likely, he was comforting her right this minute, up in Prescott. Ox went to sleep wondering if he'd ever see her again.

They went on to Tucson in four days of easy going, with the blue cardboard cutouts of the Santa Catalinas thrusting into the sky ahead, and Picacho Peak to the west and Chief Butte to the east lunging straight up out of the tremendous flat. The fluted saguaros, with their tortured, convoluted arms crowned with ivory blossoms, looked like intruders from another planet. Poppies and paint brush and nameless tiny flowers were a Persian carpet of color, and every vicious cholla and cat-claw and barrel cactus wore blossoms of incongruous beauty. Dust devils gyrated, mirages built up-sidedown castles and mountains on the horizon, and there was no single daylight hour without some sort of wheeled traffic in sight—huge, high-sided freight wagons with from ten to twenty mules, eight-mule Army jerk line outfits, a peddler's wagon, a ranch buckboard, a Mexican *carreta* with a thatched roof and sections of log for wheels, squealing along on its ungreased wooden axle, its motive power two racks of bones in the shape of mules, harnessed either side of a milk cow.

Tucson lay in its mile-wide bottom lands where the *acequías* reflected the sky between rows of willows and cottonwoods separating orchards and grain fields—the hub of a semicircle of mountains: the bold Santa Catalinas, the Whetstones, the Santa Ritas, Baboquivari Peak, the Picacho del Alamo Muerto—and, looking back, you could still see the Superstitions and the Sierra de la Estrella, seventy-five miles away.

After the war, the town had expanded from the ancient walled town, and there were now hotels, restaurants, breweries, stables and corrals, schools, churches, banks, and even a book store and newsstand. Every other business, it seemed to Ox as he rode between the freight rigs and army wagons lined head to tail on both sides of Main Street, was a saloon.

The old adobes were still there surrounding the wide plazas, the one-room mud houses with stiff steerhides for doors, and windows barred with crooked mesquite sticks. The new homes were pretentious in their flowery patios behind ten-foot walls, and the business buildings were very up-to-date, with false fronts and many-paned windows.

Ox stopped to let a train of burrows go by with their loads of olives and tobacco from Sonora, and cut in to the hitchrack of the Cosmopolitan Hotel. He had three quick ones at the bar, then got a room facing on the interior patio.

He left the Sharps rifle with the clerk, and took Lilly to Carlson's Livery Stable and Corral, down on South Meyer Street. In the same block was everything a dirty, thirsty mule skinner might desire, including women—six saloons, three card rooms, a restaurant, a barber shop, a gunsmith, a law office, a shoemaker, an assayer and a clothing store. He bought a new outfit from the skin out—longjohns, socks, a red silk shirt, copper-riveted Levi's as stiff as stove pipes, a yellow silk kerchief to tie around his neck, a flat-crowned black Stetson with a four-inch brim, and handmade boots. He took them into Greek Alex's barber shop and had a bath in the back room, and a shave. He told Alex to burn the castoffs.

For three days he just rambled around and talked to old friends. Tom Jeffords was old now, but still looked like he could fight Apaches; Estevan Ochoa had silver in his hair; W. S. Oury still lived down by Carrillo's Gardens. Ox knew Oury, but didn't go to see him. Somehow, Oury sort of made him gag. Oury had led the bloody massacre of Apache women and children at Camp Grant several years ago. A lot of people all over the territory thought Oury and the other whites and the Pimas and Papagos that had helped were heroes, and had cheered when the jury acquitted them in twenty minutes.

He went around to the corrals and freight yards and the Army Quartermaster's Corral and asked about the freighting situation. Everybody wanted to hire him. The manager at Smith's stables offered him a hundred and thirty a month. He heard, too, about the team and wagons Ed Carlson had taken in on a long overdue feed bill from some independent freighter. He went to see Carlson.

Carlson greeted him warmly. "By God, Ox! Good to see you! You gonna work out of here, now? Skinners are scarcer'n tits on a boar! Hold out for a hundred an' fifty a month!"

Ox said, "Heard you had those wagons and a good team."

"That's right! Those damn jugheads, the whole twenty, are gonna break me! All they do is eat."

Ox said, "You've got room here for the wagons, and you already have the corral. Suppose I was to drive. Suppose I was to hunt out good jobs, sort of take my pick and take the runs where there's grass and water and we wouldn't have to use up freight space carrying feed. I could work out the deals and bring the contracts for you to look over."

"For a hundred an' twenty-five a month, Ox? There's a lot to it besides just drivin'."

"Huh-uh, Ed. For a percentage of the net. Say a third."

Carlson looked at the ground and kicked a hunk of horse manure. He said, "Let's go around to Abadie's an' have a drink."

There wasn't any contract, just a handshake. Ox would get thirty per cent of the net, and that was fair because of Carlson's investment in the team and wagons.

One of Carlson's hostlers brought Ox a list of the names of the mules, and Ox had him lead them out and hitch them in their proper places along the fifth chain. The important teams, the leaders and first swingers and the pointers and wheelers, were exceptionally good. The rest of the swingers, the "fours", "six's", "eights", "tens", "twelves", and "four-teens", were as good as any skinner could ask. The off wheeler, which would be Lilly's partner, was a sixteen-hands brute named Cactus.

Ox got Lilly from her stall and put her beside Cactus, and she swung her rump and whacked him solidly in the ribs with both heels. Cactus squealed and plunged, and in a moment, the team was one big snarl of mules across the chain, kicking and bucking. Ox grabbed a halter from the fence and waded in, shouting profanity and laying about with the six-foot halter chain. Miraculously, the wild mixup settled into order, with every mule in place. Carlson came yelling out of the office and stopped short as he saw Ox laughing. "I wouldn't've walked into that fracas for a thousand gold," he said. "Looks like you're a mule man."

"That's what they were testing out," Ox said. "Ed, I ought to try 'em out on a short trip. I have to get acquainted with 'em before I take 'em on any long hauls or mountain runs."

Carlson thought it over. "Be sure they're ready to go in the mornin'. I'll ramble around town an' see what I can stir up."

Ox looked the mules over, easing up to the nervous ones, petting the quiet ones, getting them used to his voice and hands. He dodged a couple of kicks, and Jackson, the off "four", snapped at him with a clash of long yellow teeth. Ox hit him between the eyes with a right cross that would have caved in a keg. Jackson's hindquarters slumped, and he spraddled out his legs to steady himself.

"So you'll be head shy for six months," Ox told him, "but I bet you quit biting."

He set the hostler, Jim, to greasing wagons and filling water barrels, and when Carlson came back about six o'clock, they went to Huffaker's American Restaurant for drinks and supper. Carlson said, "I got a load for Nogales. Muslin and printed cottons, canned peaches, and twenty kegs of nails. Now, listen, Ox. On the way back, look for a man about five miles out of Nogales. Name's Archuleta. He'll take you to a ranch back a ways off the road, that is, he will if a certain party got the wire I sent. There'll be a load for both wagons, mostly tobacco an' barrels of olives. We get a good rate on stuff through Nogales, up from Guaymas. Saves all that distance by boat up to Yuma, and the long haul to here."

"Maybe saves going through Mexican customs, too, huh?" Ox said. "I've freighted down there before."

"Export duties never get past the pockets of them Mexican customs officers," Carlson said. "There's no dodgin' the U. S. import duties, Port of Entry's right here in Tucson, but we don't have to support them Mexicans."

Next morning when he got to the freight yard, dawn was a yellow streak over the Santa Catalinas. The wagons had been loaded during the night, and Jim was ready to go along as swamper, so long as he didn't have to get within ten feet of any mule.

The team made the turn onto Meyer Street, then right to McCormick, then left onto Main Street without acting up, but they weren't laying into the collars, just loafing along. Ox didn't want to start anything in town, with the streets already crowded and the freight rigs lined solid both sides, but he was prepared, with a halter chain within reach over the end gate of the wagon.

A mile out of town, he hit Tom, the near leader, with a stone, and swore and yelled that they were a bunch of goose-rumped goats and they'd better get a-moving. The mules kept on shuffling along with the fifth chain nearly slack. Ox reached back and got the halter chain and rattled it. Cactus lunged sideways and got his hind leg over the trace, the whole team slammed into the collars and dug in, and Cactus got dragged a few feet and skinned up a hock before he got his leg back over the trace, but he was real eager. The wagons rumbled along with the team in a brisk trot and the traces taut. Ox grinned and settled back. He'd never seen a mule team that didn't have wholehearted respect for a halter chain.

Sixty-five miles to Nogales, past the white mission of San Xavier del Bac, past the moldering remains of Tubac, a brief stop in the shade of the wall of the ruined mission of Tumacacori, past forlorn, deserted Calabasas—three days and two camps in the sweat and heat, and Ox delivered the load in the Arizona Nogales, just across the line from the Sonora Nogales.

Señor Archuleta was waiting for him outside of town, as Carlson said he would be, looking tough and dangerous on a big-horned Mexican saddle cinched onto a scrawny horse. Archuleta was primed for war, with a Colt on each hip, a machete hung from the saddlehorn, and a Winchester carbine in a boot under his right leg, with its butt sticking forward through the coils of a rawhide reata. He grinned—a gleam of gold teeth in the shadow of an immense felt sombrero, and led the wagons five miles up a steep, rocky wheel track to a corral made of mesquite sticks lashed together with rawhide. There was a scatter of eroded adobe buildings behind a nearby hill.

Ox unhitched and put the mules in the corral. The hostler stayed in the wagon until Ox put the gate poles back in place.

Archuleta said, "Welcome to my rahnch. 'Ave dreenk, eh? Come to 'house, eh?"

Ox said, "Sure. *Muy bueno. Como está usted?* You got any, le's see . . . any *cerveza, muy frio?*"

"Beer I got in well," Archuleta said. "W'y your 'elper lookin' at me like that?"

"He's scared of you, I guess," Ox said. "All that hardware you're packing."

" 'Ardware?"

"The pistols, and that carbine on your saddle."

Archuleta explained that Apaches had hit a ranch near

Calabasas, and everyone was alert. Ox said maybe they'd better get loaded, and asked where was the *contrabanda*.

Archuleta said, "My boys gonna put in wagon." He led them into one of the adobe houses, where a fat, sloppy, cheerful woman served them *tortillas* and *chorizo* and many bottles of warm beer hauled dripping from the tepid well. Outside, there was laughter and thumps and banging around, and when Ox had eaten, he went out and watched a half dozen *vaqueros* rolling barrels up a plank into the lead wagon and manhandling crates into the trail wagon. Ox asked how Archuleta was to be paid, and the Mexican said it was all arranged with Carlson.

Ox went back to the house to get the hostler, and found him still at the table, staring entranced at three objects hanging from a rafter—three small leather discs stretched on willow hoops, each suspended from a nail by a foot or more of long, black hair. When he recognized what they were, he felt his own scalp contract.

Archuleta said, "They dryeeng good in smoke from fireplace."

"Where'd you get 'em?" Ox asked.

"T'ree week ago, wass one attack on little *ranchería* over there", Archuleta said. "Wass kill t'ree woman an' t'ree kid an' one *paisano*, he's got goats. Wass Apache. One those Apache, he wass *herido*. 'Ow you say that?"

"Wounded."

"Yes. Wass wound'. Two more Apache, they helpin' him, that *herido*, so they not gone yet. We been follow weeth dog. W'ile we killin' those two, four dog wass bite that *herido*. So he's die too. We don't hafta shoot that one. W'en I'm go to Hermosillo, I'm get hundred pesos for them scalp."

"A hundred pesos apiece?" Ox asked.

"Sure. An' fifty pesos for woman. How somebody gonna find out if woman or man? One of that Apaches wass woman, but their head all same."

"That's a hell of a thing!" Ox said. "Selling the scalp of a human being! Who's the savage, you or the Apache?"

"Eh? Talk slow. How somebody gonna un'erstan' you?"

Ox said, "Come on, Jim," and went out. The hostler followed.

James Kirker, a few years ago, had delivered so many scalps to Hermosillo the Mexicans would only pay him a wholesale rate. They weren't all Apache scalps—who could tell the scalp of a Mexican from that of an Apache? And

Johnson and his partner, Gleason, had stupefied their Apache friend, Juan Jose, and fifty others, men, women and children, with whisky, and murdered them all for the bounty. But those were just stories Ox had heard—true enough, but somehow abstract, not touching him. Now he was a little sick at the stomach. He was glad to get the wagons rolling out of there.

The three days, returning, gave him a deep satisfaction with his new team, the best he had ever driven. And his beloved Lilly mule was his to have and to hold. His prospects with Carlson looked good.

As they pulled into Tucson, he saw Gwen Goodfield in the sidewalk crowd on Main Street.

chapter seven

"*Gwen!*" he bellowed, and hauled on the jerk line.

He should have left the jerk line alone. His shout scared Cactus into a semi-fit, and the leaders swung left in obedience to the pull on the line. They crashed into a hitchrack. A saddled horse broke loose and bucked across the street, scattering a file of burros like frightened quail. A cursing man on a buckboard sawed at the reins of his rearing team. Ox's mules seized the opportunity and started a free-for-all, tangling themselves in the traces. Jim, the swamper, jumped down from the trail wagon and ran into the gathering crowd. Saloon doors flapped back and forth as patrons ran out. Traffic began to pile up, and Ox caught one glimpse of Gwen, obviously startled by the uproar, running up Simpson Street.

He stared after her, but she disappeared. He ignored the uproar around his wagons—freighters in stalled rigs bawling profanity, a bartender tugging at his leg and demanding payment for the broken hitchrack, bystanders yelling advice and funny remarks. The mules were quieting down, standing every which way across the chain, head to tail and backward, snarled in the traces. He grabbed the halter chain from the endgate of the wagon and got down. In a few minutes, he had them straightened out, and drove to Carlson's Livery Stable and Corral.

Carlson greeted him and looked into the wagons. "Everything go all right?" he asked. "Where's Jim?"

Ox didn't want to admit he'd run the team off the road. He said, "He jumped off back on Main Street. Maybe he needed a drink."

Carlson grinned, "Archuleta came through, I see," he said. "After we deliver this stuff, there'll be a couple hundred dollars for you, maybe more. How were the mules? You like 'em?"

"They're good," Ox said. "Real good. Ed, I got something to do. See you tonight, maybe. Have somebody unhitch, will you?"

"Chucho Huerta can do it," Carlson said. "You go ahead."

Ox went to the Cosmopolitan and bathed and shaved and put on his new clothes and went to look for Gwen.

She wasn't in Lord and Williams store, nor Roca's Merchandise, nor the Hudson and Company Bank, and hadn't checked in at the Palace Hotel. He decided he'd have dinner, and when he walked into the Maison Doree, there she was. And there was Lew Barnes, sweating in his black suit and white shirt, grinning at her across the table.

She saw him, and smiled and waved. Lew Barnes saw him, and scowled and turned back to Gwen.

Ox blundered toward her and bumped the arm of a diner who spilled coffee and swore at him. He stood beside her, all lit up with a warm glow inside, and couldn't think of a word to say.

"Ben! How nice to see you!" Her smile was even prettier than he'd remembered. "We found out you were driving for Mr. Carlson. He said you'd be gone a few days."

"How come ... I mean ... you went to Prescott," Ox said, "and now you're ... "

"Ben, do sit down! Have you had your dinner?"

Lew's white Stetson was on the empty chair in front of Ox. Ox brushed it off onto the floor and sat down, knocking his knee against the table leg. A glass of water tipped over, and a waiter came running, and Lew swore and picked his hat up and brushed it tenderly with his sleeve. "God damn ox in a china shop!" he muttered.

Gwen frowned at Lew and he stared back at her defiantly. Ox couldn't take his gaze from her. She blushed and said to the waiter, "A T-bone, rare. And soup, and Parkerhouse rolls and coffee for the gentleman, please. Will that be all right, Ben?"

He was admiring the way her eyes crinkled when she smiled. He said, "Huh? Oh, yeah! Yeah!"

The waiter stamped away, muttering.

"What are you doing down here?" Ox asked.

"Well, Daddy didn't leave a will," Gwen said, "and the lawyer said it will take a while to get things straightened out and there weren't any jobs for me in Prescott. Lew was coming to Tucson, and said he'd find me a job here, didn't you, Lew? I don't know what I'd have done without Lew, Ben. He went with me every time I talked to the lawyer, and escorted me everywhere so ... well, so I wouldn't have any unpleasant experiences." She turned to Lew. "Do you really think . . . ?"

"I got you one already," Lew said. "I was just going to tell you when this ... when Ox barged in."

"Oh, Lew! How wonderful! Tell me ... "

"Mr. Mansfield," Lew said. "He needs a bookkeeper and somebody to help with customers."

"You mean the Pioneer News Depot?" Ox asked. He felt as if he might float right out of the chair. She was going to stay right here in Tucson! Now if only a stagecoach would roll over on Lew!

"And not only that," Lew said, "Mansfield wants you to live at his house. He said there's no decent place for a girl to stay, and his wife will be glad to have you."

Gwen looked as though she were going to run around the table and kiss him. "Why, Lew! That's wonderful! You're so good to me!"

Ox wasn't floating above his chair, now. "Why'd they run you out of Prescott?" he asked. "Thought you were going to buy up half a dozen claims or something."

"Didn't see anything that looked good," Lew said. "And Paul Connolly fixed me good. They wouldn't hire me on the California and Arizona, after that row we had in Ehrenberg."

"I hear they need stage drivers over in Yuma," Ox said. "Kerens and Mitchell. They're paying a bonus. Now, I could do you some good there, give you a letter, and ... "

Lew grinned at him. "Thanks for nothing, pardner. I'm taking the extra Overland run to Florence next Monday. And soon as they have an opening on the regular run, I get it."

Lew wiped his mouth and laid his napkin down. "Mr. Mansfield said to bring you to the house, Gwen. You want any dessert?"

"Why, I haven't even met him," Gwen said. "Doesn't it seem kind of forward to just ... "

"They're expecting us," Lew interrupted. "I'll hire a rig and we can pick up your bags at the Continental."

She got up and held out her hand to Ox, and smiled at him. "It's so nice to see you again," she said.

Ox got up too fast and knocked his chair over. Lew hurried around the table and helped her into her jacket. He paid the waiter and dropped a dollar tip on the table and they went out.

Later, in Abadie's, Ox stood at the bar, drinking morosely by himself. About nine o'clock, Lew came in, whistling. He offered to buy Ox a drink, and Ox said, "Hell with you."

Lew laughed at him, and said, "Well, the Mansfield's think she's great. She's all settled in, and grateful as hell to guess who? You gotta get there fustest with the mostest, Ox."

In the morning, Ox started out for the office of the Subdistrict Quartermaster to see if he could get some freighting business for the army, but somehow got sidetracked and found himself at J. S. Mansfield's Pioneer News Depot. He waited half an hour until Mansfield arrived, escorting Gwen. Mansfield said he was glad to see Ox back in town, and started to introduce him to Gwen.

She said, "Oh, Ben and I are old friends, Mr. Mansfield." For once, Lew wasn't there—probably sleeping off a big head in his room, wherever that was.

Mansfield unlocked and they went in, and Mansfield said, "Something I can do for you, Ox?"

Ox wasn't ready for that. He stuttered and finally said, "You got a ... well, you got 'The Decline and Fall of the Roman Empire'?" It was the only book he could think of, under pressure that way. To his disgust, Mansfield said, "Why, yes! All three volumes. Twelve fifty."

"Well, I'll just start out with Volume One," Ox said, but Gwen said, "Why, that's barely the introduction, silly!" So Ox shelled out twelve-fifty and wondered what the hell he'd do with the Decline and Fall.

While Gwen wrapped the books, Mansfield grinned at him and said, "I have an idea Miss Goodfield is going to be real good for business. Yes, sir, real good!" and Ox went red in the face, and stood around until Gwen said, "Ben, I have to work. Mr. Mansfield wants to show me the books and the billing," and Ox started out. At the door, he turned and said, "There's a real nice place over on Pennington, the Park Restaurant, with a nice patio to eat in. Can I get you about seven and we'll ... "

"Oh, Ben! I'm sorry. Lew's taking me to dinner."

Ox started to swear, caught himself just in time, and stalked out stiff-legged.

At the Quartermaster's office, he contracted for a trip to Fort Bowie, six days' drive east, with a twenty-ton load of crated rifles and ammunition, a complete blacksmith shop, and sacked grain. The going rate was eight cents a pound, but the Quartermaster didn't haggle too much over Ox's demand for ten cents—heavy freight rigs were in short supply and big demand. Four thousand dollars! And thirty per cent of four thousand, why that was twelve hundred dollars for Ox! If he made only one trip like that a month, that would be ... why, in a few months he could buy his own outfit!

He and Carlson went over to Abadie's and set up drinks for everyone, which included Lew Barnes. Lew was nursing a grandiose hangover. He said, "Gwen tells me you tried to horn in on tonight. Now, just you get something straight! I won't . . ."

Ox downed his drink and grinned. He patted Lew's shoulder and said, "Why, now, you don't *have* to take her out, Lew! I'll just tell her you had the blind staggers last night, and the thought of dinner made you heave your breakfast, and you turned her over to me."

Lew batted his hand away and walked out.

chapter eight

When Ox went to Carlson's livery before dawn, Carlson was pacing up and down and swearing. He said, "That God damn Jim quit me! Came in last night an' got his pay. We're all set to go, an' no swamper!"

"He's no loss," Ox said. "He's scared of the mules. But I can't go without a swamper."

"I sent the wagons over to the Quartermaster's Corral in the afternoon, to be loaded," Carlson said. "The team's over there, too, all except Lilly. Tell you what. Ask them for a soldier. They got some good mule men."

He went into the stable and watched Ox saddle Lilly. "She's fed an' watered," he said.

As Ox turned into Ochoa Street, he saw his loaded wagons outside the long, adobe wall of the Quartermaster's Corral, two blocks down the street. At the corner of Ochoa and Convent, a man was leaning against the wall of somebody's patio. As Ox approached, the man stepped out to intercept him.

"H'lo, Ox," he said.

"Well, for God sake!" Ox said. And after a moment, "I guess I'm not surprised."

Jake Harris's eyes had a sick look, and his hands were trembling. He said, "I got in from Prescott yesterday. Caught a ride with a freighter."

"Uh-huh," Ox said. "What'd you do to Jim Furness?"

"That his name?" Jake asked. "Talked to him in a saloon. He said he'd been swamper for you down to Nogales. I didn't *do* nothin' to him. Just showed him my bowie, an' told him I was a scalp hunter, an' his hair was black enough to pass for Injun. He said he figured to leave right away, never did like Tucson, anyhow."

"What went wrong up in Prescott?" Ox asked.

"My money run out, an' nobody'd hire me count of the booze. An' listen, Ox, I ain't had but one drink in a week. I kind of asked that Jim whatsisname some questions, an' he said you might need a swamper. I asked around, an' somebody said you had a haul for Fort Bowie."

"You quit drinkin', or you went broke, which?"

Jake didn't answer for a moment. Then he said, "I went broke." He turned and started walking down Ochoa Street.

Ox said, "Hold up, Jake. Get yourself a drink and some breakfast and be back here in half an hour."

"Awright," Jake said.

"Where's your gear?"

"Ain't nothin' but my carbine, under a pile of lumber in the corral."

Ox gave him a dollar, and by the time Jake got back to the

corral, Ox had inspected the loads and the water barrels, and hitched up the team.

A Cavalry sergeant rode out leading eight mounted troopers, and stopped by the wagons, with the troopers grumbling about the early hour, and what they'd had for breakfast, and anything else that came to mind.

"You're Davis?" the sergeant asked. "I'm Finlay." They shook hands.

Ox said, "Glad to know you, Sergeant. You keeping us company?"

"Yeah," Sergeant Finlay said. "There's fifty Springfields in them crates, an' five thousand rounds, along with other supplies. That Apache runugate's been cuttin' capers in the Whetstones. Well, you ready?"

Jake's old eyes sparkled and there was a spring in his creaky knees as he climbed into the trail wagon.

There was little traffic on the road, when they left the town—a few freight outfits serving the mining districts, a few ranch wagons—and it was dreary, hot going up the wide valley between the bald Santa Catalinas to the north and the Santa Ritas purple in the southern distance. Ahead rose the Chiricahuas, and far, far beyond, south and east, the San Ignacio range in Mexico; across the broad, grassy *ciénega*, past the turnoff to Old Camp Crittenden, on through the desolate, treeless plain to a nearly dry crossing of the San Pedro, then the long, rough grades of the Chiricahuas, 4800 feet up to Fort Bowie, which was some thirty rock and adobe buildings on the four sides of a quadrangle of fifteen acres, in an ocean of grama grass.

Captain W. Wallace, commanding Companies H and I of the Sixth Cavalry, checked the lading bills. He said his Apache Scouts had had a brush with the renegades and had killed three. There seemed to be no more than ten or twelve altogether, and they were on the run.

When Ox woke Jake up in the chill of dawn, he could hardly rouse him. He had a half empty quart clutched to his chest—probably traded some item of gear for it. Ox picked him up and dumped him in a watering trough. Jake climbed out and stood blearily repentant in a widening puddle, and Ox really cussed him out: "God damn you, I'm sick of you! What the hell good are you to anybody? Drunk or not, sick or not, you're going to handle the brake on those grades! I'm going to roll, and I swear to God, if you aren't on the job,

I'll throw you out and leave you! Now get the team and hitch up!"

Jake stumbled away toward the corral. Ox was about to smash the bottle, then changed his mind. If Jake didn't have a shot or two to steady his shakes during the day, he'd be too sick to do his job.

Almost all day, the escort had to trot to keep up. It was down grade, and the wagons rumbled around the turns with the brakes screeching. Jake was on the job—drunk or sober or hung over, he was a freighter. At the noon stop, Ox let him take a good belt of whisky. They camped that night below a pass in the Chiricahuas, and made Steele's Station the second night.

Ghosts and demons rambled around at night, and Apaches stuck to their camps and wickiups. There'd be no real danger until dawn; but, all the same, Finlay had his men on sentry-go all night. When they started out, scouts rode ahead and to each side; but this slowed progress, and about nine o'clock Finlay called them in.

The noon stop was at Croton Springs. Finlay's mount had a loose shoe, and Finlay said he was going to pull it.

Ox said, "Well, I'm going to roll, Sergeant. You can catch up easy."

"Now hold on!" Finlay said. "You're under my orders. Don't forget the Scouts found them buggers just last week."

Ox said, "Listen, Sergeant, if they're watching us, they know the wagons are empty. They'd've hit us on the way to Bowie if they were strong enough."

"They'll gamble for an easy chance t' murder you," Finlay said, "or for nice juicy mule steaks, cut off while th' critter's alive an howlin'."

Jake said, "Sarge, I fit them devils with General Crook. A little bunch like that, they won't do nothin' with you right behind us."

Ox suspected that Jake's judgment was colored by his hankering for two weeks' pay and the nearest saloon. How could Jake know it was a little bunch? But it suited his own urge to hurry back and see Gwen.

The sergeant thought it over, then said, "Well, go ahead. We'll catch up."

Two hours later, the mules were laboring up the first long grade of Nugent's Pass, with the road winding among clusters of boulders, and an arrow flitted like a streak of light past Ox's face. Pete, his near "eight", screamed and plunged ahead onto the rump of the near "six", with eight inches of arrow standing out from his ribs. The mule fell, and the others went crazy, kicking and squalling. Jake shouted something, and fired his carbine twice.

Ox hauled on the brake rope and the wagons ran off the road and stopped, canted over with their left wheels in the ditch. Somehow, he got turned in the saddle and dived over the high end gate of the wagon. There was a deep-throated "*Boom*" off to one side, and wood splinters stung his face. He grabbed the Sharps and looked over the end gate. There was a layer of smoke above a bunch of rocks, but nothing else. He ignored the pandemonium among the team.

Jake fired again, and an Apache jumped from the rocks and went up the hill at a limping run, and was out of sight before Ox could line up on him.

Up ahead, a horse burst from the brush and came at a gallop straight for the wagons. All Ox could see of the rider was an arm over the horse's neck and a leg clamped around its ribs. A rifle fired under the horse's neck, and two more Apaches charged out behind the first one. Ox swung the Sharps and fired. The running pony seemed to trip, then came crashing down and slid to a stop, hidden in dust. Ox threw the lever forward, and the empty case flipped out of the breech. He resisted the frantic urge to look at the two oncoming riders, and concentrated on reloading.

The two warriors came pounding down the road side by side. When Ox moved the Sharps into line, one of them swerved and went up the bank. The other hauled savagely on the jaw rein and his pony slid to a stop beside the horse Ox had shot down. He had a single-shot carbine in his left hand. He squalled a command and leaned down toward the still figure under the dead horse. Ox fired, and knew he had hurried it. The Apache lurched, dropped the carbine, and grabbed the pony's mane.

Ox swore and fumbled the cartridge when he reloaded. He got the shot off, but the Apache was hammering his heels into the pony's ribs, and the pony went cutting around the boulders like a jackrabbit, and Ox knew his second shot had missed.

He began to hear the squalling and yipping all around, like fifty coyotes in the brush and rocks. The demented mules were making a wild snarl of harness and spreaders and chain. An arrow quivered in the sideboard, an inch from his elbow.

He reloaded and looked around, but saw no movement. Jake fired again, from the trail wagon.

Silence and dust settled and the mules quieted down. The Apache under the dead horse groaned. Ox ignored him, watching for movement. A shout came from down the road, and the drumming of hoofs getting louder. Sergeant Finlay and a trooper went tearing by, hauled their mounts to a stop a hundred yards down the road, and looked around. They turned and came trotting back, and the rest of the troopers galloped up and stopped.

Ox climbed out of the wagon. Sergeant Finlay dismounted, and Jake came trotting up from the trail wagon.

"Anybody hurt?" Finlay asked.

"One mule dead," Ox said.

"Them son of a bitches sure got their nerve, huh?" Finlay said. "First time the whole trip we been spread out. How many was there?"

"Sounded like a hundred!" Ox said.

Jake said, "Wasn't but eight or ten."

The troopers moved around with their carbines poised, staring at brush and rocks. Sergeant Finlay said, "Le's get them jugheads straightened out an' get goin'. You hit any besides the kid there?" He pointed at the Apache under the horse. The Indian was braced on his elbows, watching them. He glanced furtively at an old Remington single-shot lying a few feet away, and tried to pull his right leg free.

His shoulder and the side of his face were scraped raw, and blood seeped from under the filthy red rag that bound his tangled, shoulder-length hair. He looked about fourteen years old, but you couldn't tell about Indians.

Ox and Sergeant Finlay and Jake walked over to him. The black eyes watched them without expression. Sergeant Finlay yelled, "Corporal! Have your men spread out. Watch the brush. You fetch your picket rope an' we'll haul this horse off the road."

Jake thumbed back the hammer of his carbine and took a step toward the boy, who stared up at him. Jake looked around at Sergeant Finlay and Ox, and said, "Well . . ." and raised the carbine.

Ox yelled, "Jake!" and grabbed the carbine, and they had a tug of war, with Jake hanging on, swearing and spitting with anger.

Suddenly, the Apache said, *"No! No me mates! No me mates!"* Ox and Jake stopped wrenching at the carbine, and looked down. The boy had twisted around and lay face down, sobbing, with his arms around his head.

Sergeant Finlay said, "Jesus! His father'd cut his throat! That sure ain't Apache style. Never saw one yet that wouldn't spit in your eye, with his hands tied an' a gun stuck in his ear."

Ox gave a sudden yank at the carbine and got it away from Jake. Jake yelled in Ox's face, "What the hell's the *matter* with you!"

"He's scared to death. Now you stop this!"

"Scared!" Jake squalled. "*Scared!* Why the hell wouldn't he be?"

Behind them, the boy said. "No Apache! No Apache! *Yo Mejicano!*" He was still crying.

"You'd *shoot* him?" Ox asked. "Just like that? A hurt kid?"

"Why, for sweet Jesus Chris' sake!" Jake said. "You ... you're crazy in the head!"

Ox let down the hammer and threw the carbine into the lead wagon. He said harshly, "Get back in your wagon!"

For a moment Jake faced him defiantly. Ox said, "Don't make me do it, Jake!" and the old man turned and stamped back to the trail wagon. The troopers, spaced out around the wagons, were scowling at Ox. The corporal spat in the dust and stared at him, hard-eyed.

Ox walked over to the boy, and Sergeant Finlay came up to them. Ox said, "I'm taking him back. You got any comments?"

Finlay said, "Hell, what's it to me? I kill 'em when I have to, but I don't hate 'em. For pure guts, nobody can beat 'em. I kind of like that in a man."

"He said he's Mexican," Ox said.

"*Si! Si! Mejicano!*" the boy said. He was watching them calmly, now, his tear-streaked face still.

"Prob'ly is," Finlay said. "They bring 'em back from Mexico, from their raids down there. I seen a lot of 'em in the old days. Murder the mothers an' fathers, an' bring the kids back an' raise 'em like Apaches. Treat 'em good, too. Just like their own kids. Well, we gotta get that pony off him."

Ox said, "Grab his shoulders. When I lift, pull him clear."

He bent down and got his arms around the dead horse's neck, and heaved upward, and grunted, "Now!" The forequarters of the horse came off the ground, and Sergeant Finlay pulled the boy free.

His filthy, too-big shirt was torn at the shoulder. There was a wide cartridge belt around his thin middle, and the shirt tails flapped loose beneath it. When he tried to stand, the long ends of his breech-clout—a piece of dirty sheet—hung nearly to the ground. His right leg gave way, and he sat down awkwardly. His bare buttock and right thigh, above the knee-high moccasin, were scraped and bleeding. He flinched away when Ox reached down and pulled the boy's skinning knife from its sheath, and took the cartridge belt.

Ox said, "I won't hurt you. You talk English?"

The boy snarled at him like a thin-faced weasel.

"*Habla Inglés?*" Ox asked.

"He'll savvy Spanish, whether he's Mex or 'Pache," Sergeant Finlay said. "They all do."

Corporal Cooper rode up and sat staring wooden-faced at the boy. Finlay said, "What you want, Coop?"

"How long we gonna hang around foolin' with that scum?" Cooper said. "*You* try sittin' out there in plain sight, expectin' a slug in th' back any second."

Finlay said, "You got any more questions, Coop?"

"Huh?" the corporal said, "How's that?"

"Git back on your post, Corporal. Just keep your eyes peeled an' your mouth shut."

Cooper's sullen face went brick red. He wrenched his horse around savagely and went clattering off behind the wagons.

"I've gotta get the team straightened out," Ox said. He turned and bawled, "Jake!" There was no answer.

"Jake!" he yelled again.

From the trail wagon, Jake yelled, "Go t' hell! You tol' me t' stay in here."

Ox swore and started for the wagon, and Jake jumped down. Ox said, over his shoulder, "Finlay, watch that kid, will you?"

It took half an hour to get the team hitched up again. They had to unhook traces and straighten out the spreaders, and hook one team to the dead "eight" and pull him into the brush. Many of the mules were skinned up, and they were all nervous as cats. Ox tied the odd mule, Pete's surviving teammate, to the back of the trail wagon.

When everything was ready, he went back to where Finlay stood watching the boy. He tried to remember his Spanish, which he hadn't used at all for two years. He said, "*Levántate!* Get up!"

The boy stared sullenly at the ground. Ox grabbed him by

the shoulder and pulled him to his feet, and he struck like a
snake and sank his teeth into Ox's hand. Ox slapped him,
hard, knocking his head sideways. "Get into the wagon," he
ordered, and gave him a shove. The boy took two halting
steps and fell. His right leg wouldn't hold him up.

Ox knelt by him and ran his hands over the foot and
ankle. The ankle was swollen to twice its size, and when Ox
tried to pull the moccasin off, the boy gritted his teeth and
tears came to his eyes. Ox pulled the skinning knife from
where he had stuck it under his belt.

"No!" the boy whispered. *"No me mates!"* He tried to
crawl away on his knees and elbows, and Ox grabbed his left
foot and pulled him back.

"Nobody's goin' to kill you," he said, and began to cut the
moccasin away. The boy sat quietly while Ox manipulated
the foot and felt the ankle. There was a bad sprain and
maybe a torn ligament.

"Jake, come here!" Ox ordered, and Jake walked over.

"You ride with him in the lead wagon," Ox said. "If he
acts up, we'll tie him. Make him behave, huh? But if you
hurt him, Jake, you'll regret it. You'll regret it in a hospital,
and that's a promise."

Jake turned loose his dammed-up anger. "You're a fool!"
he snarled. "What you think you're doin', anyway! That's a
murderin' Apache. Tried t' kill you! Jesus God A'mighty, Ox,
knock him in the head, same as a rattler!"

"Listen, Jake. He's Mexican. Most likely they killed his
folks and raised him for an Apache. He don't know any
better."

"How many you s'pose he's murdered a'ready?" Jake demanded. "You're goin' agin your own folks, Ox. Apaches
ain't human! They're dirty, creepin' murderers, an' that's *all*
they are!"

"Maybe they got their reasons," Ox said. "Get in the
wagon, or I leave you here!"

"You'd never do it, Ox!"

"Try me!" Ox challenged.

He was greatly relieved when Jake climbed up on the
wheel and got in. The boy offered no resistance when Ox
picked him up and helped him to climb in. Jake stuck his
head out and said, "What about the brake? Who's gonna . . . ?"

"We've got level going the rest of the day," Ox said. "I'll
worry about the brakes."

Ox drove all afternoon with the crawly feeling up his back

that Apaches were behind every rock. The troopers flanked
the wagons, and Sergeant Finlay rode point, a quarter of a
mile ahead, and Corporal Cooper rode rear guard, a hundred
yards back.

They made camp well out on an open flat, and Finlay
picked his men for sentry duty. None of the troopers would
speak to Ox, and Jake made his attitude clear by building a
fire away from the wagons, and cooking for the troopers. Ox
unhitched and waited a few minutes, trying to get the boy to
talk to him. The boy wouldn't speak to him.

Ox said, *"Vente! Vente conmigo!"* His Spanish, such as it
was, was coming back to him. Somewhat to his surprise, the
boy limped along after him as he went to the fire. He stopped
outside the ring of seated troopers. Finlay was eating from a
tin plate, off to one side.

"Jake," Ox said, "the mules aren't watered. That's your
job."

Without turning from the fire, Jake said, "I quit my job."

Ox started for him, and a trooper stuck out his foot and
tripped him. Ox stumbled and almost went down. He recov-
ered and turned. The trooper had laid his plate down and
was getting up. Ox kicked him in the shin. The trooper
squawked and fell over, clasping his shin. Corporal Cooper
and the four troopers who were not standing watch got to
their feet. Sergeant Finlay went on with his meal.

Ox strode toward Jake, who started to back around the
fire. Ox took two long steps and got him by the collar. He
said, "Go water the mules! When that's done, take your
carbine and bed down under a wagon. You stay awake. All
night! I'll check, and I better not catch you asleep. You got a
bottle?"

Jake clamped his jaws together and wouldn't answer.

Ox knotted his fist in Jake's shirt front and shook him, with
his head snapping back and forth. Jake was trying to answer,
now, but Ox kept on shaking him. When he stopped, he said,
"Have you got a bottle?"

Jake gulped, and gasped, "Only—only a couple drinks left
in a pint."

"Break it," Ox ordered. "Right now! I want to hear it." He
shoved Jake, who stumbled away.

There was a sudden uproar among the mules, a squeal, a
thump, and a yelp of pain. Ox ran to where they were
bunched around Lilly, in the dusk. The boy lay groaning on
the ground. A halter rope with a snap hook on one end lay

near him. If it had been horses, he might have got away, but not with those man-eating mules. Ox picked him up and carried him to the fire. There was a raw scrape and a blue bruise on his ribs. If the hoofs had caught him square, he'd be dead.

Ox called Jake from his task of watering the mules. Jake came promptly. "You break that bottle?" Ox asked.

"Yes, God damn it! Your ears plugged up or something?"

"All right, Jake. Tie the kid's hands, and tie him to a wheel on the trail wagon. You'll be on watch all night. If he gets away, or anything happens to him, from you or anyone else"—Ox looked around at the troopers and went on: "including Corporal Cooper, you'll regret it. You believe that, Jake?"

"Yeah," Jake said. "He ain't gonna git away."

The boy stood quietly as Jake tied his wrists.

Corporal Cooper ran a finger around his gums and spat. He walked around two troopers and stood in front of Ox. Ox looked him over—six feet or more, chunky, solid, bullet-headed.

Cooper hitched up his belt and said, "Mister, I didn't sign up to play nurse to no mother-lovin' Apache. You're a squaw-humpin' son of a bitch."

Ox ignored him. He yelled, "Jake! Do what I told you! And finish watering the team!"

Jake came back to the fire, leading the boy. He said, "Huh-uh. I'll stay an' watch you get your fat head kicked in." He sat down and hauled on the halter rope to pull the boy down beside him.

Sergeant Finlay said, "Coop ain't got good sense. The rest of you keep out of it. That's an order!"

Cooper turned to look at Finlay, and Ox hit him so hard his head and shoulders struck the ground while his feet were still in the air. He went over in a complete backward somersault and lay sprawled, face down.

Jake was on his feet, doing a little jig, his eyes shining in the firelight. "I *knew* it! I *knew* you'd take him!"

Ox was inspecting his split knuckle when the corporal groaned and rolled over. He got to his knees, braced himself on his arms, and shook his head slowly. When he managed to stand and take a step, he dropped to one knee, and got up again. His walk back to the fire was erratic.

Sergeant Finlay looked up from his plate. "You got your wits back?" he asked Cooper. "Can you understand me?"

The corporal spat blood and worked his jaw back and forth with his hand, and muttered, "Yeah."

"You're first on sentry," Finlay said.

Ox went to the wagons. The boy was sitting under the trail wagon tied to a rear wheel, with his wrists tied behind him. Jake was finishing watering the mules. Ox got his blankets and wrapped one around the kid, and stretched out under the front of the wagon, with the Sharps within reach.

A trooper woke him before daylight. The boy still sat huddled under the blanket, apathetic and sullen. Looked like he'd sat there all night without moving. Near him, Jake was flat on his back, snoring. Ox shoved him with his foot.

Jake said, "Wha ... What?" and scrambled to his feet and bumped his head on the reach. "Guess I went t' sleep," he mumbled.

Ox said, "Of course you went to sleep. What else? Bring in the team and water 'em and get the feed box down."

"Well, Jeez, Ox," Jake said. "I mean, a feller's gotta git some rest."

"Shut up!" Ox said. "Get moving!"

When Ox untied the boy's hands, he felt sorry for him. He could hardly move his arms, and his hands were swollen.

No one spoke to Ox during breakfast. When the team was hitched, Sergeant Finlay rode up to Ox and said, "That kid sure don't want to go with you. Maybe you oughta turn him loose."

Ox said, "It's not right to let him grow up like a wild animal. He's going to have a chance at a decent life, not grow up in a brush wickiup eating lizards."

"Whether he wants it that way or not, huh?" Finlay said.

"Whether he wants it or not," Ox answered. "How's he ever going to know anything different if he doesn't get the chance?"

"How's it feel playin' God?" Finlay asked.

"Name it anything you want," Ox said. "Just keep your nose out of it."

For the next two days, everyone rode alert and nervous, but nothing happened. The kid, tied in the trail wagon where Jake could watch him, still wouldn't talk. He limped only a little, now.

On the outskirts of Tucson, Sergeant Finlay rode up beside Ox and motioned to him to stop. He said, "Better keep the kid under cover goin' through town. Lot of folks think 'Paches ain't human. Somebody might get hot headed."

"Guess you're right," Ox said. "Tell Jake, will you? Tell the kid, too."

Finlay dropped back to the trail wagon and talked to the kid in Spanish too fast for Ox to follow.

The troopers turned up the street heading for the Quartermaster's Corral, and Ox pulled into Carlson's yard just as the sun went down.

chapter nine

Ed Carlson came out of the office and watched the wagons swing in from the street. He called to Ox, "Lost a team, huh? What happened?"

"Half of it's tied on behind," Ox said. He hollered "Whoa," and climbed stiffly down from Lilly.

A couple of hostlers came from the barn and began to unhitch. Jake walked around from the trail wagon and said, "Ox, can I git paid?" He was pulling the boy along with him.

Carlson gaped at the dirty Apache clout and the lank Apache hair, and exclaimed, "For God sake, what's *that*? An' who the hell are *you*?"

The hostlers were staring at the Mexican boy, and Ox said, "Come into the office, Jake." He took the boy by the arm and said, "*Vente*," and the boy limped along with him.

Carlson sat down at his desk, and Jake said, "Ox . . . "

"Shut up!" Ox said. "Ed, this is Jake Harris. I picked him up for a swamper the morning we left. He's worked for me before. Good mule man."

Carlson looked Jake over and didn't say anything, so Ox went on, "He's got thirteen days coming at two-fifty. Let's see, that's . . ."

"Thirty-two fifty," Carlson said. "Is he goin' to work regular with you?"

"I don't think so," Ox said, but Jake didn't hear him. He was watching Carlson open the petty cash box. Carlson handed Jake the money, and Jake stood his carbine in the corner and hurried out.

When Ox had told the story of the Apache attack and the rescue of the Mexican boy, Carlson asked, "What did you bring him along for?"

"Well, God sake, Ed! He's Mexican. Would you have just left him?"

"I'd've shot him," Carlson said. "He's Apache now. What the hell you gonna do with him?"

Ox hadn't thought out any answer to that one. "Why, hell, I don't know," he said, "clean him up, get him some clothes, maybe see he gets a chance to go to school."

"What for?" Carlson asked, and Ox began to get sore. He wished he'd never seen the damn kid.

"Listen!" he said. "If you don't like it, Ed . . ."

"Le's not go into that," Carlson said. "What you gonna do with him right now, tonight?"

"Well, maybe bed him down in the stable till I can . . ." Ox began, and Ed said, "Not here. I won't trust him around the place. An' you don't think they'd let him into your hotel, do you—long hair, no pants, Indian stink all over him? Haven't you got any idea what they think about Apaches in Tucson?"

"But he's not Apache!" Ox exclaimed. "That's exactly the point!"

"Sure as hell looks Apache to me," Carlson said. Suddenly, at the top of his voice, he shouted, "*Chucho!*" Ox jumped, and the boy made a grab for Jake's carbine. Ox spun him around and held him against the wall.

A middle-aged Mexican came in. He hesitated, and Carlson said, "Come on in, Chucho." The hostler sidled across the room without taking his eyes from the boy.

"He's s'posed to be Mexican," Carlson said. "Ask him some questions."

Chucho said, "He's Apache. Maybe he's talk Spanish, but he's Apache."

"Find out, anyway," Carlson ordered, and Chucho began to question the boy; and suddenly the boy's eyes filled with tears, and he began to talk, the words tumbling out all mixed up with his blubbering. He talked for ten minutes, and before he was through, Chucho had his arm around him, and was sniffling, too.

The boy hiccuped and blew his nose on his fingers. Chucho said, "He's Mexican, Mr. Carlson. Eight, nine year ago w'en he wass only five year, he's live in Chihuahua. Then those Apache, they hit that ranch an' kill ever'body. They burnin'

up ranch an' they takin' him an' he's sister, only she's holler
an' cry an' they knock her on head. An' Apache what take
him, he's Juan Pedro, an' Juan Pedro take him like he's own
boy an' raise him up. They stayin' on that White River
reservation, an' ever'body's think he's Apache. An' w'en he's
get big enough, he's go some time with Apache w'en they
jump ranch or something, but they only let him hold horses
back in⁻ chaparral. This time, w'en they jump Mr. Ox's
wagons, he's gonna show he's big fighter, so he's run out on
horse in front of ever'body, an' Mr. Ox shoot he's horse."

"How you know he ain't lyin', Chucho?" Carlson asked.

"He talkin' good Mexican, better than Apache talk, an' he's
tell true story, ever' little thing, names, place w'ere something
happen. An' 'nother thing, he's cry. Apache don't never cry,
not if you take hour to kill 'em. Even Apache baby don't cry.
Mr. Carlson, this good Mexican boy. He's have bad time."
Chucho patted the boy's shoulder.

"What's his name?" Ox asked.

"Manolo," Chucho said. "Manolo Contreras."

The boy said, "Apache, they callin' me 'Flaco', 'cause I got
skinny arm an' leg. But I'm plenty strong, me."

Carlson grinned, and Ox said, "Well for God sake!"

Flaco said, "I livin' eight year on White River reservation, I go many time to San Carlos Agency. I talkin' good
Englis'."

"Well, listen, Manolo, Flaco, whichever you are," Ox said.
"What are you going to do, run off the first chance you get?"

"Oh, I'm not run away," Flaco said. "I'm tired livin' in
chaparral, alla time hungry, an' ever'body wanta kill you."

"Chucho," Carlson said, "you got any room at your
place?"

"Sure, Mr. Carlson. Only five kids home now. He can stay
there."

Ox said, "I'll pay his board. How much?"

Chucho put on a bargaining expression, sort of sharp and
innocent all at the same time. He said, "Five dollar a week?
'Cause I gotta buy extra food an' we don' got enough
blanket, an' ... "

Ox got twenty dollars out of his wallet and said, "Here.
For the first week. Get him some clothes with the rest, and
make him take a bath."

Chucho grinned. "Nex' time you see him, he gonna be nice
clean Mexican boy, not smell like wil' animal."

"Get his hair cut," Ox said.

"Come on, Flaco," Chucho said. He took the boy by the hand. In the doorway, the boy held back and looked at Ox.

"No cut hair!" he said vehemently.

Ox slept late. At breakfast in the Maison Doree, somebody asked him about the attack on his wagons, and others crowded around his table, and the waiter said anybody that spared an Apache's life ought to be run out of town. Jake must have really shot off his mouth last night. The story now had it that fifty warriors had jumped the wagons and Jake and Ox had stood them off, and it was only because Ox had grabbed the chief's son as a hostage that they'd got through alive.

When Ox went to the livery stable, Carlson said, "Why'n't you take a day off? Talk to the merchants and the Quartermaster. Stir up some business."

Ox said, "We can put the old nigh wheeler in place of Pete as Maude's team mate—you know, the one I replaced with Lilly. And, Ed, I have to tell you—Jake Harris is a good man, savvies the mules and all that, but he's a boozer. So if you know of a good swamper, maybe we better . . ."

"Good swampers are hard to get," Carlson said. "You better hang onto him."

"Well, just so you know about him and the booze," Ox said. "Where's Chucho live? Thought I'd see how the kid's getting along."

"He's got an adobe shack on Calle de la Guardia. Ask for Chucho Huerta."

Ox stopped by the book shop, and Mansfield said, "I hear you're running a one-man Indian rescue mission."

Gwen greeted Ox with a smile. She said, "I think it was wonderful, what you did. Everyone knows about it, how you and Jake fought off the whole band until the cavalry came, and how you wouldn't let the Apaches take that poor Mexican boy, and fought the corporal to protect him. I'm proud of you, Ben!"

Jake's mouth sure must have been loose last night!

Ox thought he'd better strike while the iron was hot. "Can I pick you up for dinner tonight?"

"Oh, Ben, I'm sorry!" And she really looked sorry. "But Lew is due in with the Overland stage from Florence and we're going to dinner."

Mansfield said, "Gwen, I really ought to get those letters in the mail," and she said, "I have to get to work, Ben. Will you bring the boy to see me?"

Disconsolately, Ox started for Calle de la Guardia to find Chucho Huerta's house. Owen Mason, Sheriff Charley Shibell's deputy, stopped him as he crossed the Plaza de las Armas. "Good to see you back, Ox," Mason said. "I hear you and Ed Carlson got a deal goin'."

Ox said hello.

Mason said, "Ox, about that Apache kid . . ."

"Owen," Ox interrupted, "when I do something against the law, you step in. But till I do . . ."

"Hold on, Ox! Hold on, now! I'm not . . ."

"He isn't Apache," Ox said. "He's Mexican. Mexicans built this town a couple hundred years before you got here."

"I know," Mason said. "Chucho Huerta says he's Mexican. But by God, he don't look Mexican, even in the clothes Chucho bought him. He's lucky somebody didn't down him on his way to the California Store. People were starting to get ugly, and if I hadn't walked 'em home, there'd've been trouble. You can't blame folks, Ox. Too many of us have fought them bastards. It's that hair down to his shoulders."

Ox said, "You gonna hang him 'cause he wears his hair long? Maybe you oughta get out a warrant for Wild Bill Hickock and Bill Cody."

"Don't get funny with me," Mason said. "You're askin' for trouble. Why'n't you send him to the reservation?"

" 'Cause he's not Apache," Ox said, "and he's got as much right here as you have."

Ox moved on across the Plaza, and Mason kept pace with him. The deputy said, "Well, for God sake then, make him cut his hair an' keep outa sight till folks forget about him."

They turned into Calle de la Guardia, and Mason swore and began to walk faster. A block farther on, a man was pounding at the door of an adobe house. There were two others with him. The deputy yelled, "Hey, there!" and two of them walked hastily around the corner.

The one hammering on the door had hair down to his shoulders, and Ox said, "My God, Owen! Long hair! Let's lynch him!"

"Very funny!" Mason said. And to the long-haired man, "Who you?"

"You know what they got in there," the man asked belligerently. His hair was greasy under a shapeless hat. His eyes were set too close against his red, bulbous nose. His mouth was a small red pout. Ox remembered the repulsive features and the filthy clothes, the low-hung Colt and the quilled, Plains Indian vest with the gold watch chain running from pocket to pocket—one of the two buffalo hunters in the saloon in Ehrenberg that had been ready to jump into the fight when Lew Barnes and Paul Connolly went at it.

"Who you?" the deputy asked again. "Haven't seen you around."

"Name of Tully," the man said. "Mike Tully."

"He's a buffalo hunter," Ox said. "They all smell that way." He pinched his nose between thumb and forefinger.

"So me an' Skin Deschamps had a big winter," the hunter said. "Three thousand hides delivered to Rath an' Wright in Dodge. So we come south for a little rest. Anything wrong with that?"

"Only one thing," the deputy said. "Keep your nose outa other folks' business."

"You know what they got in here?" Tully demanded. "A 'Pache buck! People ain't gonna stand for that, Sheriff!"

Ox said, "Listen, Greasy! He isn't Indian, he's Mexican. And Chucho didn't bring him to town, I did. So *I'm* your man, you son of a bitch!"

"I ain't forgot you," Tully said. "You was lookin' for trouble that time in Ehrenberg. You'll likely find it. Now . . ."

Mason said, "Get away from here, Tully. Don't come back."

Tully started to bluster, but something in the deputy's demeanor stopped him. He walked away.

Mason knocked on the door and said, "Open up, Huerta."

The door creaked open, and Chucho said, "Ever'body makin' trouble. My wife scared."

She looked it, too, there behind Chucho with her huge black eyes rolling in her plump brown face. The five kids behind her were crying. Back in the gloom of the room, Flaco sat on a tumbled, swaybacked bed, in stiff Levi's and a gaudy shirt. He wore a cheap sombrero, Indian style, with no dents in the crown, and the brim flat as a board.

They went in, and Mrs. Huerta herded the kids into the adjoining room.

"Damn it, Chucho," Ox said, "I told you to get his hair cut. With short hair, nobody'd give him a second look."

"He wou'n't do it!" Chucho said. "I tol' him, an' he wou'n't do it!"

"Well, by God, he will!" Ox said. "Flaco . . ."

"No!" Flaco said, with his thin jaw set.

"Now, you listen, kid!" Ox moved toward him and Flaco scuttled into a corner and stood defiant. Ox began to drag him toward the door, and Flaco ducked his head down and bit him on the wrist. Ox swore and slammed him back against the wall.

"No cut hair! No cut hair!" Flaco was almost hysterical.

"Not Apache, huh?" Mason laughed. "There's two things no Apache will do. Won't eat fish, it ain't clean or something, an' won't cut their hair. Takes all the strength out of a warrior, same as if you cut his balls off."

"Well," Ox said, "maybe I'm rushing things. He's just fresh out of the *chaparral*, like a trapped coyote."

"Sure," Chucho agreed. "He stay with us, eat good beans an' chili, bimeby he's forget that Apache business. Mr. Ox, I'm better stay home today. You tell Mr. Carlson, eh?"

"You got a gun, Chucho?" the deputy asked.

"Yeah, look." Chucho dragged a long double shotgun from under the bed, an old cap-lock Enterprise. "She shoot everything, buckshot, solid *bala*, li'l pieces of scrap iron."

"Well, keep it handy. Don't open up for anyone you don't know."

The deputy walked away with Ox when they left. He said, "It'll quiet down. It's only fools like Tully and a few others. If you'd get the kid's hair cut . . . "

The deputy went off about his business, and Ox thought he'd better talk with Mansfield. Mansfield struck him as sensible, not one of those hotheads that hated all Indians with blind malevolence. As he rounded the corner, he saw the sign in front of Welisch's White House, and remembered that Welisch Brothers also carried on an import-export business from their warehouse on Nutter Street. He crossed over and went into the store.

The Welisch's had staple groceries and eight tons of wool in 150-pound bales for Hermosillo, down in Sonora, but every freight outfit in town was busy. If Welisch could get the goods to Nogales, a Mexican outfit would take it on to Hermosillo. Ox said he'd take it for ten, if he didn't have to deadhead back, empty. Herm Welisch said he'd send a letter, and arrange for a load of hides and tobacco to come back. Ox said he'd have the wagons there in the morning for loading, and leave the day after.

Mansfield looked a little sour when Ox walked into the Pioneer News Depot.

"What's your trouble?" Mansfield asked. "Path of true love a little rocky?"

"It's the Mexican kid," Ox said. "I didn't know what I was getting into. Guess I thought everyone'd be glad to see a kid get away from the Apaches. You'd think I dropped a sidewinder in people's lap!"

Gwen came in from the back room.

Mansfield said, "Well, he *was* with those Apache murderers. Back in '70 and '71, they hit the stage stations at Cienega and Picacho, and murdered everyone there. And just three years ago, a big party of Mexicans were killed, men, women and children, coming back to Tucson from Nogales. Tortured and murdered. And all through the war, the Apaches ran wild, nothing to stop 'em. You can't really blame folks, Ox."

"Well, yeah," Ox said. "But he's just a kid. He didn't know any better."

"I don't feel like some others," Mansfield said. "If you like, I'll talk to Otero. You know him? Fine man. Big family. They might take him in."

"Thanks very much, Mr. Mansfield. Trouble is, right now he's in Chucho Huerta's place, and Chucho's watching the door with a shotgun. They're scared to stick their nose out. And I'm leaving for Nogales, day after tomorrow."

Mansfield said, "Why don't you take him with you? Give people a chance to forget him. In the meantime, I'll talk to Otero."

"You hit it!" Ox said, grinning.

Gwen said, "This is a fine thing you're doing, Ben. I'd like to meet your protege. I'll help all I can."

"Why, you can help *me* right tonight!" Ox said. "We can have dinner at . . ."

"Oh, Ben! I *told* you! Lew will be back from Florence."

Ox's spirits fell flat. As he headed for the door, she called after him, "Tomorrow night, Ben? And after dinner you can take me to Mr. Huerta's and I can meet the boy?"

"You betcha!" Ox said, and went out with a spring in his step.

When he walked into the office, Carlson said, "Some damn buffalo hunter's blowin' around the saloons he's gonna hang up your hide to dry, along with Flaco's scalp."

Ox turned around and started out. "Where is he? I should've broke his back this morning!"

"Hold on!" Carlson said. "The way I heard it, Owen

Mason told him he'd put him under bond if he don't quiet down. He was just drunk an' blowin' off."

Ox told him about the trouble at Chucho's house, and Carlson looked half mad. He said, "I told you that kid would be nothin' but trouble! Now Chucho can't come to work an' you spend the day wet-nursin' an Apache brat. Good for business, huh?"

"Listen, Ed!" Ox said. "We didn't sign any contract. We'll chop it off right now!"

"Oh, cool down!" Carlson said. "I went over to see Etchells, over at the wagon factory. He's got a load of steel, been sittin' in Yuma ten days for lack of transportation. If you get off your ass and dig us up a load for Yuma, we got a good job."

"That's a miserable haul to Yuma," Ox said. "You've got to haul water and mule feed, it's a real mule killer."

Carlson got sore again. "Well I be God damn! You're s'pose to find the jobs, and you spend all your time doin' good to murderin' Apaches and chasin' that girl! An' here I . . ."

Ox began to laugh, and said, "I got a full ten-cents-a-pound load for Nogales and a full load back! You better buy me a drink!"

Carlson punched him on the shoulder and said, "I'll buy you ten drinks! Come on!"

They had a drink in Abadie's and one in the Fashion Saloon and another in the Hole in the Wall. Jake Harris was in the Hole in the Wall, drunk and noisy, and was very hurt when they wouldn't let him join them. Ox looked for the greasy buffalo hunter, and the more he drank, the more he wanted to find him; but he wasn't in any of the saloons they patronized as they slowly worked their way to the Park Restaurant.

They were working on their after-dinner brandies when an uproar broke out at the Butterfield Overland Station, just across Calle de la Mision—people yelling and running around. The diners all rushed out.

People were milling around a stagecoach, and before Ox and Carlson got there, Owen Mason and another deputy came charging up on horses and got down and shoved their way through the crowd to Lew Barnes, who was talking to the manager under the lamps at the station door.

Bystanders were clustered around three gesticulating pas-

sengers. Ox bulled his way through with Carlson at his heels,
and heard Owen Mason ask, "How long ago?"

Lew Barnes mopped his face with a bandanna. "Maybe
two hours. Not five miles out of the last station."

"How many was there?" the deputy demanded. "You get a
look at 'em?"

"It was getting dark," Lew said. "One of 'em let go a shot
over my head. I pulled up, and Billy Mayo swung his shotgun, and somebody back in the brush hit him with a carbine."

Inside the station, there was a man stretched out on the
counter, and several men around him, and Doc Wilbur came
in through the back door and said, "Make way there!"

"The one I saw had a handkerchief over his face," Lew
said.

"Did they get the box?" the manager asked.

"What d' you think!" Lew said. "Me up there like a duck
on a rock with Billy bleedin' in my lap, an' that one out in
front with a gun on me, and another back there in . . ."

"God damn!" the manager said. "First one in eight
months!"

"Anything else you can tell me?" the deputy asked.

"It was almost dark," Lew said, "and I . . . well, he said
throw the box down and drive on, and that's all I could do." •

"That's right!" one of the passengers said. "Just like he
said, the man said throw it down and . . ."

"Well, I'll get out there," Mason said. He and the other
deputy mounted and the crowd let them through. Several
men ran for their horses and spurred after them.

The manager said, "Come on in, Lew. We'll write a
report."

"God damn it!" Lew exploded. "There wasn't a thing I
could do! If you think . . ."

"I'm not blaming you," the manager interrupted. "We
don't want our drivers playing hero." He went inside.

Lew started in and saw Ox, and stopped and said, "Listen!
Gwen's expecting me. Tell her I'll be there. An hour,
maybe."

The liquor was churning around in Ox. He decided he
didn't really like Lew Barnes worth a damn. "Why, just never
you mind," he said. "*I'll* take her! I'll tell her a little man
popped outa th' brush an' said 'Boo!' an' you threw that ol'
Wells Fargo box right at his head, but your horses ran away
with you an' you couldn't stay an' fight!"

Lew's green eyes narrowed to slits. He said through clenched teeth, "You fat-mouth son of a bitch!"

The manager called from inside, "Barnes? Come in here, will you?" For a minute, it looked as if Lew were going to start something, but he turned and went in.

Carlson said, "I'd've thrown the box down. So would you."

In Abadie's, an hour and three drinks later, a man standing beside Ox at the bar said to his companion, "The son of a bitch prob'ly was in on it himself. Easiest thing in the world, you take a driver he's got a couple friends an' he knows when he's gonna be carryin' a fortune in the box. An' they plug the shotgun guard to make it look good."

Ox was ashamed of what he'd said to Lew. He swung around and said, "Friend, by any chance, are you referrin' t' my frien' Lew Barnes, you son of a bitch?"

The man wasn't as tall as Ox by half a head, but he wasn't scared. He looked Ox over and said, "You're drunk," and turned away.

Ox grabbed him and turned him around. He came around swinging, and got Ox right in the eye. Ox howled and swung, and missed. Carlson got him by the collar, but Ox brushed him off. The man punched him in the mouth. The bartender came around the end of the bar with a sawed-off billiard cue and said, "Not in here, gentlemen!"

Men were crowding around three deep, and Ox got the man by the lapels and dragged him through the swinging doors onto the boardwalk. He ignored the punches and held him off and cocked his fist, and from the street a woman's angry voice said, "*Oh!*"

Ox looked up foggily, and there was Gwen in a buggy with Lew. Lew bowed and saluted him with a flourish of the whip. Gwen stared straight ahead, and the buggy rolled down the street and disappeared out of the fan of lantern light.

The man punched Ox behind the ear. Ox twisted him off his feet with one hand and flung him face down onto the boards.

The grinning ranks closed around him. He started to push his way through, and one big man thought he wouldn't move out of the way. He stood with his fists on his hips and said, "Don't shove, you 'Pache-lovin' bastard! Just don't shove *me!*"

Ox shoved him in the face with all his weight behind it. The big man's head clunked against the door frame. He slid down to a sitting position. Ox stalked away into the dark.

chapter ten

Ox woke up late. The taste of his mouth gagged him, and his head felt three heads big. When he went down the hall to shave and saw himself in the mirror, he groaned. His right eye was yellow and purple, and he had a split lip. He shaved carefully, leaving the stubble on his upper lip.

When he went to Carlson's livery after breakfast, Carlson was in as ugly a temper as Ox. He said, "How long you gonna have Chucho watch-doggin' that God damn 'Pache kid? An' who's payin' him?"

Ox said, "I'll pay him. He'll be back on the job tomorrow. Now I'll take the wagons over to Welisch's, if you're through runnin' off at the mouth."

"Why'n't you lose the kid down there?" Carlson said. "Let him go back to Mexico. An' where's that God damn drunk swamper of yours? Don't he work for his pay like the rest of us?" He went out and hollered for the hostlers to hitch up.

When Ox swung the team into the street, Carlson climbed into the lead wagon. He said, "I wanta see Herm, get the lading bills straight."

Ox stopped the rig in front of Welisch's warehouse on Nutter Street, and as he got down from Lilly, Gwen and Lew Barnes came along. Gwen was neat in the white blouse and plain jacket she wore at work. She was going to sail right by, but Lew came up to Ox and scowled and said, "Let's hear you say that again, what you said about me in front of everybody over at the Butterfield Station."

Ox was about to tell him to go to hell, but he was really ashamed of himself. He said, "I didn't mean it. I had a few too many."

Gwen was staring up the street as if she were alone in the world, but she said, "Humph!", and Lew grinned. Carlson got down from the wagon.

"All right," Lew said. "Forget it. Looks like you got stomped by a bull buffalo. What were you celebrating?"

Gwen said, "He doesn't need an excuse. He just hits whoever is closest, and it's always somebody smaller than he is." She still wouldn't look at Ox, and he wished she'd move on. And if Lew didn't quit grinning, he was going to give her another sample of how he could slug someone.

Lew said, "What started it? Somebody else doesn't like your cozying up to a dirty Apache kid?"

Ox growled and started to grab him, and Carlson said, "Some shorthorn at the bar was tellin' the whole room he figured you rigged that holdup, Lew, and Ox knocked him down. An' if I was Miss Goodfield here, I wouldn't be so damn fast jumpin' to conclusions." Carlson went into the warehouse.

Gwen stared after him, with her face getting red, then turned to Ox, and said, "Oh, Ben! I'm *sorry*! I thought, well, we saw you and . . . oh, I'm so sorry!"

He said, "You mean if I slug somebody that says something about Lew, why that's all right. Is that it?"

"No!" she said. "You *know* that's not it!"

"Well, you tell me, then," Ox said.

"Oh, Ben! It's just that . . ." she stopped and looked as if she were about to cry.

"Aw, let's forget it," he said. "See you tonight? Seven o'clock?"

"Seven is fine," she said, and smiled, and suddenly it was a beautiful morning. Then she spoiled it by turning to Lew. "You can come, can't you? You won't be driving?"

Lew grinned and said, "Why, sure! Damn nice of you, Ox."

"And after dinner," Gwen said, "we're going to see that poor Mexican boy."

"Well," Lew said, "not me, I guess. I don't want to see him. Might forget myself. I drive coaches, and Indians shoot 'em up and murder the passengers. Maybe you forgot."

Gwen's face went white. Ox said, "Why, God damn you!" but Gwen hung onto his hands and said, "No, Ben!"

Lew turned away and said, over his shoulder, "You coming, Gwen?"

She looked at his back and said, "No, Lew, you go ahead."

Lew shrugged his shoulders and walked away.

Ox walked with her to the book shop. They didn't say anything until she went in, when she smiled and said, "See you at seven, Ben."

When he got back to Welisch's warehouse, roustabouts had

started loading. Ox unhooked the chain, and Carlson said, "Ox'll be here with the team early in the morning, Herm."

After they drove the team back to the livery stable, Ox spent the morning checking over harness and gear and, after lunch, searched the saloons until he found Jake, half sober. He said, "I'm leaving at six A.M. If you're not at Welisch's warehouse, I'll leave without you."

"If I ain't there," Jake said, "you could pick me up at that IXL boarding house. It's at . . ."

"I'm not picking you up," Ox said, and walked out.

He went to his room and cleaned up and put on his good clothes.

He went to the Pioneer News Depot at closing time, and Mansfield told him his eye looked like the chromo of Sunset over the Colorado River, on the wall.

Gwen came from the back room and said, "Now, Mr. Mansfield! Don't joke about it. He was defending Lew Barnes against a vicious lie."

Mansfield said, "Perhaps he could find a worthier cause." He locked the door behind them and walked off down the street.

Gwen, looking startled, stared after him. Ox said, "Maybe I ought to just take you home. I guess I don't look like the perfect lady's escort."

She said, "You look fine to me, and what others might think doesn't concern me. You're a pretty fine man, Ben, helping that boy and standing up for Lew. I just wish . . ."

"What?" he asked.

"Well, just that everything didn't have to be settled with fists."

In a nearly womanless town, everyone stared at Gwen wherever she went. Ox resented it whenever he was with her, but tonight, at dinner, most of the stares were for him, and most of them were amused.

Later as they strolled north on Church Street, along the ruined wall that surrounded the old Mexican part of the town, Gwen said, "Lew says the boy—Flaco, is it?—is really Apache. He says you ought to turn him over to the army. I think, whether he's Apache or not, you did a fine thing, but I hope it isn't going to make trouble for you."

They turned left onto Calle de la Guardia. "He says he hasn't got any folks left in Mexico, or I'd try to send him back," Ox said. "There's a Mexican down by Nogales, fellow named Archuleta. Maybe I can put Flaco with him."

Ox knocked on the door of Chucho's shuttered house. It opened a crack, and Chucho's worried face appeared behind the shotgun. He said, *"Pasen ustedes!"*

Chucho pushed a ten-year-old boy out of the only chair in the cluttered room. Three smaller children, who had been squealing in some roughhouse game on the bed, stared solemnly at Gwen as she took the chair. Mrs. Huerta, plump, blowsy and pretty, peeked around the door of the other room, where a charcoal *brasero* smoked under a clay pot.

Ox said, "Gwen, this is Chucho Huerta."

Chucho responded with a courtly bow. Mrs. Huerta bobbed her head and pulled it out of sight. A naked, dirty, two-year-old boy made his way to Gwen and stood at her knee, fingering one of the mother-of-pearl buttons on her skirt. Gwen picked him up and set him on her lap.

"Where's Flaco?" Ox asked.

"Flaco! Asómate!" Chucho said, and Flaco emerged from the kitchen stuffing half a *tortilla* into his mouth. His new clothes were already dirty. He stood chewing with his mouth open, staring at Gwen.

"Saluda a la sénorita!" Chucho ordered. "Whatsamatter you? Say hello to lady!" Chucho turned to Gwen and said, "He ignorant."

The unblinking stare began to anger Ox, but Gwen smiled and said, "How do you do, Flaco." Then, to Ox, "Does he know any English?"

Flaco stopped chewing long enough to say, "Spick Englis' good, me."

"Mr. Ox," Chucho said, "las' night two men go by on horse. They shootin' gun in air an' holler, 'Dirty Apache sonabitch'."

"Who?" Ox said. "Was it that Tully, the one yesterday?"

"I can't see 'em good," Chucho said. "But today, I go for grocery, people on street tell me he gonna kill us all in bed. Some Mexican, they tell me I better sell his hair down at Hermosillo. I'm scare' leave house an' go to work."

"What do they mean, sell his hair?" Gwen asked.

"Scalp. Mexicans, they pay for Apache scalp. Hundred pesos for one scalp," Chucho explained.

Shocked, she turned to Ox. "Do they really . . . ?"

"Some used to make a business of it," Ox replied.

"Oh, Ben. How *could* they! How could anybody . . ."

"I don't know either," Ox said. "Chucho, I'm taking him

with me, tomorrow. Got a run to Nogales. You go back to work in the morning."

Chucho's face showed relief. He said, "Awright, that good. I give you back three dollar from he's board money. I got four dollar lef' from buyin' clo'es, too. Here." He fumbled at a pants pocket.

"No, keep it," Ox said. "You've been off the job two days, and I don't think Carlson will pay you. Can you bring him to the yard about daylight?"

"Sure!" Chucho said, and broke into rapid Spanish, to which Flaco listened intently. Chucho turned back to Ox and said, "He be there."

Ox said, "Well, then. Gwen ... ?"

She put the infant down, looked ruefully at the dirtied front of her dress, and got up. She held her hand out to Chucho and said, "It's very nice of you to help Flaco, Mr. Huerta."

"He good boy," Chucho said. He shook her hand and said formally, *"Mucho gusto, Sénorita."*

Suddenly, Flaco grabbed Gwen's hand, and pumped it up and down. His wide smile showed his teeth surprisingly white in the frame of thin, dark face. He said, "You nice lady! How do!"

"Why, thank you, Flaco! I think you're a very nice young gentleman!"

Flaco turned to Chucho. "What she said?" he demanded. Chucho rattled off some more Spanish, and Flaco grinned still wider.

As they left, they heard the bar slide into place behind the door. Gwen said, "Flaco's really in danger, isn't he? I'm glad you're taking him, but what about when you get back?"

Ox said, "I'll try to figure something out while I'm away."

Ox was up at four A.M. After breakfast, he found Chucho hitching the teams to the chain, and Flaco helping, agile as a monkey, talking to the mules, not afraid of them. "Good job, Chucho," Ox said. "You teaching Flaco the business?"

"I don' teach him nothin'," Chucho said. "All Apache know plenty 'bout horse an' mule."

Ox mounted Lilly and motioned for Flaco to mount Cactus, alongside. The boy scrambled up, and Cactus laid his ears back and shuffled his feet. Flaco batted him alongside the head and said, *"Cálmate,* sonabitch!"

"By God!" Ox laughed. "The complete muleskinner."

The team didn't want to go, and it took some cussing and

a few cuts with the blacksnake before they surrendered to the inevitable and shuffled through the gateway. With a hand on the jerk line, Chucho walked beside the nigh leader, through the dark and silent streets. Ox appreciated this, because the bark of a dog or a sheet of newspaper moving in the dawn breeze might set the team off, and there were no wagons hooked on to curb their enthusiasm.

The loaded wagons waited in front of the warehouse, and Jake Harris stood talking with Herm Welisch under the lantern above the door. Ox got down.

Roosters were crowing and the blue night over the Santa Catalinas was giving way to a fan of pale lemon light. Flaco scrambled nimbly over the doubletree and came to stand beside Ox.

Welisch handed Ox several papers and said, "Here's the lading bills." He looked at Flaco and said, "I heard about him. Some folks think you're a damn fool, Ox."

Ox folded the papers and put them in his wallet. He said, "If you're one of 'em just keep it to yourself."

Up to now, Jake hadn't said a word. Now, he said, "Is he goin' with you?"

"He is," Ox said.

Jake said, "Well, Jake Harris ain't! Jake's gonna git drunk."

Ox stared into the malevolence of Jake's old eyes, then turned to Chucho. He said, "I'll write a note to Carlson, tell him you're going to swamp for me this trip. Go tell your wife. Hurry it up, huh?"

Chucho ran up the street.

Ox asked Welisch, "Can I get a piece of paper in your office?"

When he came out with the note, Flaco was standing at the head of the nigh leader. Jake wasn't there.

Chucho came back and got into the trail wagon. Ox and Flaco mounted and Ox hollered at the team and got them going. He turned into Meyer Street and stopped on the corner of McCormick long enough for Chucho to take the note into Carlson's office.

Chucho seemed to be taking a long time, and Ox was about to get down and find out why, when he heard him trotting up to the trail wagon. In a moment came the shouted "Yo-o-o!" and Ox slashed at the rumps of his "fourteens" with the blacksnake and swore at his leaders, and the wagons rolled.

The first day's run was flat as a table top, with no need for braking. Chucho was probably asleep on the bales of wool in the trail wagon. Ox pulled off the road for the noon stop.

He got down and Flaco stepped onto the wagon tongue between Lilly and Cactus, and vaulted over Lilly and landed like a cat. He grinned and was in the middle of saying something unintelligible, when his face went still and expressionless. He was staring over Ox's shoulder, and Ox turned, and there was Jake walking up from the trail wagon. He wouldn't look Ox in the eye. He said, "I'll unhitch."

Ox said, "Where's Chucho?"

"Back at Carlson's. I told him I was goin', not him."

"How many bottles did you bring along?" Ox asked.

"Not none!" Jake said, and started toward the lead team to unhook.

"You come back here!" Ox yelled, and Jake turned and came back.

"You'll agree to one thing," Ox said, "or you'll walk back. You think I mean it?"

"Yeah. What is it?"

"You won't say a word to the boy, not one, the whole trip."

"I'll go unhitch," Jake said.

Both night camps were crowded with skinners and swampers visiting each other's fires, and Flaco stayed out of sight, in a wagon. Jake ignored him, and even when he got high enough on borrowed drinks to get real mouthy, he said nothing about the boy.

It took a full day in Nogales to drop off the cargo and load the hides and tobacco. Jake disappeared, and Ox, alert for trouble, kept Flaco with him; but there were Indians in town, Yaquis and Pimas, most of them long-hairs, and the boy was not conspicuous. After dark, Jake came back, only half drunk. The three slept under the wagons, in Ortega's freight yard.

In the afternoon, three miles north of Nogales, they met Archuleta riding in to town. He looked as villainous as Ox remembered. He glared at Flaco, who stayed up on Cactus while Ox dismounted. Archuleta said, "Where you got that 'Pache sonabitch?"

"He isn't," Ox said. "He's Mexican."

"He 'Pache!" Archuleta insisted. He drew a long breath through flared nostrils. " 'Pache! Archuleta can *discernir* . . . How you say that?"

"I don't know what the hell you're talking about," Ox said.

"By nose!" Archuleta said. He touched his great beak with a forefinger. "By nose, I tell 'Pache from Mexican. He 'Pache sonabitch!"

Flaco ripped off a string of Spanish and spat in Archuleta's direction.

Archuleta roared with delight. "You hear?" he said. "You hear w'at he's call me? He's call me one lard-ass Cholo pig with bad smell! He Mexican, you bet!"

Flaco began to grin and dropped lightly to the ground. For ten minutes, Ox had to sit and listen to a gabble of Spanish. Before it was over, Archuleta was wiping his eyes on a dirty sleeve. He grabbed Flaco in a bear hug and said to Ox, "*Pobrecito*! Poor li'l *chamaco*! He's got no *papá*, no *mamá*! All kill by them sonabitch 'Pache. He's say you he's papa, now." He pushed the boy away, and before Ox could dodge, he was in that bear hug, with Archuleta's stubble rasping his cheeks one after the other, and the stench of bad teeth and *sotol* gagging him.

Jake grinned for the first time in four days, and said, "I be damn'! Love at first sight!"

"You hear 'bout them 'Pache bastard?" Archuleta asked. "Them soldier from White River, they trap 'em in *barranca*. *Zas! Zas! Zas!* They kill six them bastard. 'Pache scout from them reservation. Pretty good, eh? 'Pache kill 'Pache. They kill their own *mamá* if they got chance."

"They get 'em all?" Ox asked.

"No," Archuleta said. "Some get away on foots. Get out of them *barranca* where them soldier he can't go."

Flaco came over from the wagon. "*Mataron a Juan Pedro?*"

"No. *Se escapó ese bastardo*," Archuleta answered. He explained for Ox: "Sonabitch Juan Pedro, he's got away. Somebody wass shoot him in shoulder, li'l while ago. But he's got away."

"Was he the one?" Ox said to Flaco. "That day we picked you up?"

"Sí," Flaco said. "Juan Pedro."

"You know that one?" Archuleta asked.

"I shot him, myself," Ox said.

It was the afternoon of the second day when Flaco got interested in buzzards, a whole flock of them, circling over the creosote brush where there was a clump of palo verde a half mile off the road. They passed a rough wheel track branching from the road, angling off toward the trees. Flaco pointed with his chin and said, "Dead mans."

Ox said, "Those Apaches got you spooked. Probably a cow."

Flaco jumped down and said, "I catch up, me." He began to trot down the wheel track, and Ox yelled, "You come back here," and stopped the team.

Jake came trotting up from the trail wagon with his carbine and said, "What's up?"

"God damn kid!" Ox said. "You set the brake?"

"Yeah," Jake said, gazing after Flaco's jogging figure.

Ox got down. "Hobble the leaders," he ordered, and got the Sharps from the wagon. He started at a fast walk after Flaco, and in a few minutes, Jake caught up with him.

Jake said, "Two span of oxen came along here. Pullin' a *carreta*. An' look here, horses cut in from th' side."

They began to get the stench, sickly, almost tangible on the hot, still air. Up ahead, a dozen buzzards floundered into the air. A million flies were buzzing. Under the trees were a brush shelter with two water skins hanging from its short posts, a clumsy, big *carreta*, four dead oxen and six dead Mexicans—two men, a woman, a young boy, an older girl, and a naked girl child, all torn by the beaks, hideous and bloated. They had all been scalped.

"Juan Pedro!" Ox said.

"No Juan Pedro," Flaco said. "No Apache!" He turned the body of the baby over. Below the bloody mess of its head was a bullet hole, a round, blue hole between the miniature shoulder blades. Ox turned away.

"Kids shot," Flaco said. "Big people get killed with knife."

Jake picked up an empty whisky bottle and smelled it. He held it out to Ox, but Ox shoved his hand away. Jake said, "Can't tell. Prob'ly arsenic in the whisky."

"Let's go," Ox said, and walked back down the track. Jake and Flaco trotted to catch up.

"That wasn't 'Paches," Jake said. " 'Paches don't take scalps. Not like Comanch' an' 'Rapahoe an' Pawnee, an' them. An' 'Paches wouldn't've just killed 'em quick, the'd've had their fun with the knives an' the hot coals first."

At the wagon, Ox said, "Jake, wrapped up in my coat . . ."

"Hell, Ox," Jake said, "I already found it. But, honest to God, I only took three drinks, one last night an' two this mornin'."

When Jake brought the pint bottle, it was still three-quarters full. They lowered it considerably before they drove on.

chapter eleven

It was late when they pulled into Tucson, and only the night watchman was at Welish's warehouse. They left the wagons there and drove the tired team to Carlson's livery. Carlson was waiting for them, and he and Ox watched as Flaco went about unhitching the mules. Jake fidgeted, then couldn't wait any longer. He said, "Mr. Carlson, I got seven days comin', and . . . "

Ox said, "You got six days coming. You spent the day in Nogales in the saloons. Now, help the kid." Jake grumbled and got to work, and Ox and Carlson went into the office. Carlson rolled a cigarette and asked, "Trip go all right? Any trouble?"

"No trouble," Ox said, "but we saw a hell of a thing. Still gives me the heaves." He told Carlson about the murdered and scalped Mexican family.

Carlson said, "They were sayin' around town the Apache Scouts had caught up with that God damn Juan Pedro."

"According to Jake and Flaco, this wasn't Apaches," Ox said. "They said Apaches don't take scalps."

"Well, I be damn," Carlson said. "Scalp hunters workin' again." He dropped his cigarette and stepped on it, and went on, "The quartermaster's office paid us for the haul to Bowie. You got ten hundred an' eighty dollars comin'. You wanta see the breakdown, the expenses?"

"Hell, no!" Ox said. "Whatever you say." It was more money than he'd ever seen in one piece.

Jake came in and got his fifteen dollars and put his carbine in the corner and hurried out.

Ox said, "What the hell am I gonna do with Flaco? I guess I got a bear by the tail."

"Well," Carlson said, "tonight anyway, why don't you an' him sleep in the barn? We'll talk it over in the mornin'."

Carlson sent his night man to the Maison Doree to bring supper to Ox and Flaco. Ox and the boy spread blankets on the hay in the barn.

When they had eaten, Ox watched him roll in the blanket and squirm around for a comfortable position. In the lantern light, Flaco looked like a young girl, with his long hair rumpled around his face and the long black lashes lying on his cheeks . . .

Ox said, "I'm going out a while. You stay here."

Flaco raised his head. "Eh?" he said.

Ox said, "Lemme see . . . *no salir*, huh? Don't go out."

Flaco grinned. "*No salgo*," he said. "I gonna sleep, me."

Ox walked to the nearest saloon—the Hole in the Wall in Gay Alley—for a nightcap. Lew was at the bar with two men. One was Tully, of the long hair, the loud mouth and the beaded vest with the gold watch chain across it. The other was just as dirty, just as long-haired as Tully, but tall and scrawny, with long, yellow, horse teeth that overhung his lower lip in the tangle of beard—the one that had been so eager to jump into the fight in Ehrenberg with his bowie knife, until he'd seen Ox ready to smash him with the chair.

Lew said, "Hey, Ox! Want you to meet a couple friends of mine from Ehrenberg. Tully there, and Skin Deschamps. Skin's gonna ride shotgun messenger for me. I fixed him up with the Butterfield manager. Billy Mayo's still in the Army hospital."

Tully said, "I met him. Man that likes 'Paches."

"You the one?" Skin Deschamps asked. "I hear the kid's got a real head of hair. Sort of walkin' investment on the hoof, huh? Worth a hundred pesos."

"Yeah," Ox said, "and squaw hair's worth fifty. I'll remember that mop on your skull, in case I need fifty pesos."

Deschamps thought it over. "Why, you God damn . . . !" He took a step toward Ox, thought better of it, and stopped.

"God damn what?" Ox said, and waited.

Deschamps muttered something and turned back to his drink.

Ox walked out.

In the morning when Ox got up, Flaco was already working with Chucho Huerta, forking hay down from the barn loft.

Ox waited until Carlson came about eight, and told him,

"I'll have to do something about Flaco today. Find him some place to stay. I'll talk to Mansfield."

Carlson said, "He can stay around here till you get him fixed up. My help's all Mexican, they'll watch out for him."

"Thanks, Ed," Ox said. "Thanks a lot."

He went to his hotel and cleaned up and shaved and put on his good clothes. After breakfast, he went to the Pioneer News Depot. Gwen, fresh and sparkling, greeted him with a big smile and told him Mansfield wouldn't be in until later.

She said, "I've had news from Prescott. The court is about to release Daddy's estate to me, and the lawyer himself made me an offer for the mine and the stamp mill parts, too. Isn't that wonderful!"

Ox didn't think it was so wonderful—waiting for some such settlement was all that was keeping her in Arizona, so far as he knew. He said, "Maybe you ought to get some other offers first. Have somebody look the mine over and tell you what it's worth."

"Well, I just don't know yet," she said. "Lew says . . ." She paused. Lew again! Always Lew! He wished Lew would drop dead! She went on, "And, Ben, the lawyer said they haven't caught those Indians, the ones that . . . that held up the stage." Tears came, and she looked away from him.

Chucho Huerta came in. He swept off his broken-brimmed sombrero and greeted Gwen, and said to Ox, "Mr. Carlson got hurry up job. You gotta come now."

Ox said, "I'll see what it is, Gwen. Will you tell Mr. Mansfield I was in? I wanted to ask him if the Otero's will take Flaco."

"Yes, Ben. He's concerned about the boy." She walked to the door with him.

Carlson had a rush job—a crusher for the Gold Tree Mine twenty miles up into the Santa Ritas out of Calabasas, a four-day round trip.

With only one wagon, there was no need of a swamper to brake the trail wagon, so Ox decided not to take time to find Jake and sober him up. Flaco was ecstatic when Ox told him to come along.

As he swung the team onto Pennington Street, Jake lurched out of a saloon. He yelled at Ox and broke into a clumsy run, but Ox touched up the team with the blacksnake and pushed it into a trot. The old man followed all the way to Main Street. The last Ox saw of him, he was leaning against a wall, gasping for breath, old and forlorn, with his thin shoulders slumped. Ox was hard put not to stop for him.

They got back to Tucson about seven P.M. the fourth day. Chucho Huerta was there to help unhitch. He said he'd take Flaco home with him so Ox wouldn't have to stay with him and sleep in the barn.

"Well, thanks, Chucho," Ox said, "but don't get into any trouble."

When they had gone, Ox walked over to the Maison Doree and looked in to see if maybe Gwen was there with Lew. If she was, he'd go and clean up and come back. But he didn't see them, so he went in and had three drinks and dinner, and went to the hotel.

As he walked in, the night clerk said, "Hey, Davis! You know Mansfield, he's got the Pioneer News Depot? Wants to see you in the morning."

He went to the book shop right after breakfast. Gwen was smiling, looking extra radiant—probably over that offer for the mine in Prescott. Ox was glad the spells of dejection over her father's murder were lessening.

Mansfield came to the door of the back room and said, "Morning, Ox. Come on in here."

When Ox was seated across the table from him, Mansfield said, "Ox, I'm afraid that kid's in real danger. I talked with Owen Mason. He's had a few complaints, but he's not worried about the people that come right out and squawk to him. It's others around town, a bunch of hot heads with not enough to keep 'em busy. There's one fellow, name of Tully, keeping things stirred up."

"He's the one tried to make trouble at Huerta's place," Ox said.

"Well, anyway, I talked to Jose Otero. He's got relatives all over Sonora. He's going down there in a week or so, and if some of them will take the boy, we can send him down there."

"Why, that's fine!" Ox said.

"Well, we've got to do something with him until then," Mansfield said. "I talked it over with Mrs. Mansfield. We have a Mexican cook and gardner, and he can stay with them."

"Mr. Mansfield, that's a big relief to me!"

"That's all right, Ox."

On his way back to Carlson's Livery, Ox bought a shirt and Levi's and a suit of longjohns for Flaco. Couldn't deliver him to Mansfield's greasy and dirty with that wild Apache stink on him.

Flaco was delighted with the new clothes. In the barn, he peeled off the dirty ones, and Ox got a tub and filled it with water. Skinny and dirty, Flaco held up the new longjohns to admire them. His ribs showed, and there was no fat to soften the lines of lean, tough muscles.

"Take a bath first," Ox ordered.

"Eh? Bath?" Apparently the word was not in Flaco's vocabulary.

"*Lavarse,*" Ox explained. "*Bañarse.*"

"*Lavarme? Por qué lavarme?*" Flaco was genuinely puzzled.

"Get in the tub," Ox ordered.

He found a bar of naptha soap and a grimy towel in the office. Mute and unhappy, Flaco allowed himself to be scrubbed. Ox was unhappy, too, particularly with the tangled, rancid mop of hair. He soaped it again and again, and poured bucket after bucket of water over Flaco's head.

Flaco dried himself after a fashion and put on the new clothes. Ox said, "Tonight you're going to Mr. Mansfield's house."

Flaco just looked dumb. "Massfeel?" he said. "What that?"

Ox said, "You're going to stay where Miss Goodfield lives. As soon as your hair's dry, we'll go to the barber shop."

"Bobber shop?"

"Get your hair cut," Ox said.

Flaco understood that, all right! He made a rush for the door, and Ox barely blocked him off. "No! No cut hair!" Flaco's black eyes rolled. He wasn't putting it on, he was really scared.

Ox held on to him and said, "Now cut that out! That's just an Apache superstition! You're Mexican!"

"No cut hair!" Flaco wailed, struggling in Ox's grip.

Outside, Carlson yelled, "Ox! Hey, Ox!"

"All right," Ox yelled back. "Where's Chucho? Send him in here, will you?"

Flaco's eyes were darting around like birds in a net. Chucho came in and said, "You want me?" He grinned at Flaco and said, "Hey! You pretty! *Muy guapo,* eh?"

Ox said, "He's spooked. Don't let him get away, huh?"

Chucho said, "Sure. He stay." And to Flaco, "Wassamatter, you scared? *Cálmate!*"

Two men were talking with Carlson in the office. One, a

grizzled old-timer in range clothes, said, "Mr. Davis? I'm Benson. U.S Deputy Marshal. This is Mr. Ogden. He's with Pinkerton. We've been looking into that stage hold-up where Mr. Goodfield and Mr. Ford were killed. Been working around Ehrenberg and Prescott. We want to check on the one here a couple of weeks ago, too."

Ox shook hands with the beefy man in the neat suit and the derby hat. "You find out anything?" Ox asked.

"Not much." Ogden said. "I understand you got to the scene first."

"Yeah," Ox said. "Me and Jake Harris."

"Used to know Harris," Benson said. "Damn good man, only I hear he's punishin' the bottle. Heard he claims it wasn't Indians hit that coach."

"I'll find him," Ox offered. "Might have to sober him up."

"We'll talk to him and Miss Goodfield later. What's your opinion, white men or Indians?"

"I go along with Jake," Ox said. "I figure someone wanted it to look like Indians." He told about how the harness had not been taken, about the shot-open Wells Fargo box, how the pistols had been taken from the dead men but not the cartridges.

"We found the coach horses," Benson said. "They just drove em off a few miles an' turned 'em loose. I figure Injuns would've kept 'em or ate 'em."

"You know anything about that Butterfield hold-up here a while back?" Ogden asked.

"Well, I saw the coach when it came in, but that's all I know. The driver said it was getting dark and somebody shot Billy Mayo, that's the shotgun guard, and . . ."

"We already talked to the Butterfield manager. Lew Barnes was drivin', huh? Wasn't he at Ehrenberg when the other happened?"

"Yes," Ox said. "He said it was Indians. We argued about it."

"How about that Tully and Deschamps? Were they in town here, too, when Barnes got held up?"

"Why, yes," Ox answered. "I think they were."

"I understand the bald headed one—that's Deschamps, huh?—I hear he's gonna ride shotgun guard for Barnes," the Marshal said. "They were hangin' 'round Ehrenberg, too, weren't they?"

"Yes," Ox said.

"Uh huh. Well, thanks, Davis. You think of anything else, look us up. Where'll we find Miss Goodfield?"

Ox told them, and went back to the barn. By God, it was possible! Those two hunters were capable of it!

Chucho was watching Flaco as the boy sat sullenly on the upturned bucket. He said, "Mr. Ox, maybe you oughta not cut he's hair yet. He scared, you know?"

"Well, I guess it doesn't matter right now," Ox agreed. "He'll be staying at Mansfield's for a while, till Mr. Otero arranges for him to go to Mexico. Keep an eye on him, will you? Get him some supper, and I'll be around for him about five thirty."

Ox went to Hand & Foster's Saloon for a drink before going to his room to clean up. He wasn't surprised to find Jake in the saloon, only partly drunk. You might walk into any of the twenty or thirty saloons any time and find Jake. Jake's feelings were still wounded. He borrowed ten dollars and said, "I s'pose you're gonna take on that God damn 'Pache kid for swamper. Don't give a damn if ol' Jake starves, huh? After all I done for you."

Ox said, "Who the hell's got time to sober you up every time I start a trip?"

He told Jake about the U.S. Deputy Marshal and the Pinkerton man. "They'll be looking you up," he said.

"I'll put a flea in their ear," Jake said.

"What flea?" Ox asked.

"Tell 'em to take that God damn Lew Barnes somewhere an' beat it out of him. They don't need to look no farther."

"Now, listen here!" Ox began.

"Where's he get all the money he loses to them two buffalo skinners playin' poker?" Jake said. "Not on no hundred an' twenty-five a month. Why's he so damn anxious to make everybody think it was Injuns killed Gwen's father? An' what about Tully an' that son of a bitch Deschamps? *They* was there in Ehrenberg. An' now they're down here, thick as fleas. An' Deschamps ridin' shotgun for Barnes. Who got him the job? Barnes did! Nice set-up, huh? They both know when they got a Wells Fargo box full of payroll or bullion. Don't think it ain't been done before!"

"You're just shooting off your mouth," Ox said. "You'll blab around, then *they'll* beat it out of *you!* Serve you right, too."

"Oh, yeah?" Jake downed his drink. "Well, I'll lay you odds that holdup of Lew two weeks ago ain't the last one!

Him an' Skin Deschamps'll come rollin' in hollerin' hold up, with the coach shot up, an' tell everybody what heroes they was, but the box'll be gone! You mark my words!"

"Listen, you damn fool!" Ox said. "*Somebody'll* mark your words! Somebody'll leave you face down in an alley!"

"Awright," Jake said. "Listen, Ox," his voice went plaintive, and there were tears in his faded blue eyes, "you givin' me th' go-by? You gonna have that Injun kid swampin' for you?"

"No," Ox said. "I had to take him last time 'cause there was no place to leave him. He's not safe around town. He's gonna stay at Mansfield's, till we can make some permanent arrangement."

"Then, you mean . . . can I . . . ?"

"Yeah, I guess so," Ox said, "but for God sake, cut down on the booze some, will you? And show up at the livery and do some work. Carlson's gettin' sore about you."

Dressed in his best, shaved and shining, Ox stopped by the livery for Flaco at quarter to six. Sullen and downcast, Flaco had nothing to say as they walked to Mansfield's house.

Gwen greeted them and made much of Flaco and was rewarded with a reluctant grin. She led them into the living room. Plump and pretty Mrs. Mansfield smiled and patted Flaco on the shoulder. Mansfield talked to him in fluent Spanish, but drew no response.

In the midst of an awkward silence, there was a knock on the door. Mansfield answered it, and ushered Lew Barnes into the room. Lew was dressed to the hilt, with a diamond stickpin in his immaculate shirt, his boots polished, his suit pressed. The gun on his hip was new, a nickel-plated Colt with carved ivory grips.

His grin faded when he saw Flaco. Gwen put her hand on his shoulder with a familiarity that made Ox wince. She said, "Now, Lew! Flaco's going to stay with us a while."

"Right here in the house?" Lew demanded. "Why, that's . . ."

"Of course not!" Mrs. Mansfield said. "He'll live with Concha and Ernesto, out in back. John, bring them in, will you?"

Mansfield went out through the dining room, and presently came in with the cook and the gardener. Concha, fat, perspiring and motherly, took Flaco's arm. Ernesto grinned and nodded to the boy. Concha said, *"Venga, hijo!"* Flaco threw one accusing look at Ox and gave in to the tugging on his arm. The three Mexicans went out by way of the kitchen.

Lew Barnes said, "You're making a mistake, Mansfield. A dangerous mistake. I'd as soon carry a sidewinder in my pocket. Never trust an Apache!"

"Slight error in nationality," Mansfield said. He wasn't smiling. "He's Mexican. And when I want your advice, I'll . . ."

"Now, Papa!" Mrs. Mansfield intervened.

"Well," Lew said, "what risks you take with your own family are none of my concern, but when it comes to Gwen . . ."

"Since she's not a member of *your* family," Mansfield said icily, "just mind your own business."

"Papa!" Mrs. Mansfield squeaked.

Lew turned to Gwen with a big grin, and she gave him a smile of such radiance, Ox wanted to slap her. And slug Lew right in those shiny teeth.

Gwen said, "I'll get my jacket," and went down the hall. Ox was struck with a dismal foreboding he didn't want to examine. He said, "Mrs. Mansfield, anything the boy needs, you know, clothes and such, why you let me know."

Gwen came back in with a silly-looking hat pinned on top of her handsome head, and wearing a jacket pinched in at the waist and flaring out over her round hips. She danced up to Lew and clasped her gloved hands around his arm and said, "Let's take Ben with us."

"Why certainly! Certainly!" Lew's grin threatened to split his face. "I'll buy him the best dinner they've got!"

Gwen took Ox's arm and tugged the two men toward the door. She called over her shoulder, "I may be late!"

Lew had a rented surrey waiting, and to Ox's way of thinking, Gwen sat a lot closer to Lew than the width of the seat required.

Lew pulled up in front of the Park Restaurant. As he helped Gwen down he said, "I ordered a private room. Come on, Ox!"

The table had tall candles and a bouquet of flowers. Lew ordered champagne. An obsequious waiter brought it in an iced, silver bucket, and poured with a flourish. Lew said, "Tell the cook we have a guest. We want three dinners, like the two I ordered."

"Yes, Sir, Mr. Barnes! It'll take a while."

"No hurry," Lew said. He grinned at Gwen and she smiled resplendently. Ox didn't want to know why they were so happy, he only wanted to leave.

Lew lifted his thin-stemmed glass. "A toast, Ox! A toast to my . . . well . . . to Gwen, huh?"

Gwen didn't raise her glass. She reached across the table and took Ox's great clenched fist in her hand. Her face was serious, almost tender. She said, "Ox, we haven't told anyone else. You're the first . . . "

Somehow, Ox raised his glass, and only spilled a few drops down his shirt. He choked on the champagne and grabbed frantically for his handkerchief. Miserably he dabbed at his shirt front. He couldn't look at her. He knew if he looked at Lew, he'd slug him on that gloating grin. He tried to say "Congratulations!" and couldn't get it out.

There were tears in Gwen's eyes. She looked beseechingly at him and said, "Ben! Tell me you wish me happiness." He mumbled something.

Later, tossing on his bed in the hotel, he remembered the rest of his ordeal . . . Gwen's exclamations when Lew took the jeweler's box out of his coat pocket and put the diamond ring on her finger, Lew asking maliciously if Ox wanted to be best man, his own struggle with the lobster, Gwen's merriment, and her alternating compassionate looks at him, and finally, his mumbled excuses and ignominious retreat and Lew's laugh as he walked blindly out of the restaurant.

The thought of Gwen married to that spendthrift, loose-living son of a bitch was unbearable. Dawn was a faint gray in the east before Ox slept. He woke at eight and shaved and dressed, and went to the Hole in the Wall and downed three drinks. Jake was snoring on a bench against the wall.

At nine, he went to the Pioneer News Depot. Mansfield barely nodded and went into the back room. Gwen smiled brilliantly and said, "Hello, Ben."

"Can you step outside for a minute?" he asked.

She followed him out to the street. She said, "Mr. Mansfield will hardly speak to me. He said Lew wants to marry me for the money I'll get for the mine. Why are people so hateful!"

Ox said, "He's right," and her face flamed, then went white. She turned toward the door, and he grabbed her arm.

"He's no good!" Ox said, and she tried to pull free, but he held on.

"I won't listen!" she said. "Let go of me!"

"You'll listen!" he said, with his jaw clenched. "Where do you think he gets the money for diamond rings and stick-pins? On a hundred and twenty-five a month?"

She jerked her arm furiously.

"How do you like the company he keeps?" Ox said. "Those two stinking buffalo hunters. How come they're always around when somebody sticks up a stage?"

"What are you trying to say?" she demanded. "It was Lew that was robbed!"

"Sure! Big hero! But *somebody* got the money, all the same. They were all in Ehrenberg when your father was murdered."

"You're too cowardly to face *him*!" she broke in. "Sneaking to me, behind his back! Well, don't worry, I won't tell him. He'd kill you!"

"Maybe you don't know," he said, "there's a U.S. Marshal and a Pinkerton detective asking about him."

"Yes, I know!" she said. "They came yesterday with their sly questions, their dirty hints! I told *them* what I think of them, *believe me*!"

"Gwen, listen to me!" he pleaded. "You can't do this! Wait! Think it over!"

"Do you think I don't know what's driving you?" Her face was almost ugly with anger and contempt. "Do you think I haven't seen you slobbering over me, fighting yourself to keep your hands off me? You pitiful dumb ox!"

He let her go. She stood with blazing, tear-brimming eyes, glaring her scorn. Suddenly she hit him in the face as hard as she could swing her hand, and ran into the shop.

Ox went through the rest of the day like a sleepwalker, hardly aware that, for once, Jake Harris showed up fairly sober and worked hard all day. He responded to Jake's one attempt at conversation with a growl of such savagery that Jake thereafter kept quiet. Ox and Jake and Chucho took the mules, a few at a time, to Tom Belknap's blacksmith shop for shoeing. The mules gave enough trouble to keep Ox busy and he quelled the fractious ones with a harshness that approached brutality. Chucho kept a nervous eye on him as though he were the rear end of a mule.

Late in the day, when they brought the last of the mules back from Belknap's, Carlson told him, "We've got a full load for Florence. Dry goods and farm tools. Welisch is sending the stuff over in a dray. I'll stick around and see that it's loaded tonight."

Ox grunted something and turned to go.

"You hear me?" Carlson demanded. "What the hell's chewin' on you?"

"I heard you," Ox said, and kept on walking.

"Now you listen!" Carlson said. "You been like a bear with a sore ear all day. This is business, an' you can damn well leave your personal troubles out of it!"

Ox turned slowly and grated, "Keep your nose out. And your mouth shut!"

Carlson flushed red, and they were having a kind of staring contest when Jake, looking nervous, tried to sidle past Ox.

Ox caught his arm and stopped him. "Be here at six in the morning!" Ox said. "And be sober!"

Jake stood quiet until Ox let him go.

Ox didn't bother to wash up or go to the hotel to change his rank clothes. He went to the Maison Doree and snarled at the waiter and choked down a meal. He thought he'd better get drunk if he wanted to get to sleep tonight.

If Gwen had told Lew what Ox had said to her, Lew was most likely looking for him. Lew's favorite hangout seemed now to be the Hole in the Wall, where he played poker with Skin Deschamps and Tully, so Ox went there. Lew wasn't there, nor were the buffalo hunters. Ox sat at a corner table and drank until midnight. It seemed as if the liquor wasn't getting to him, until he got up to leave. As he wove his way among the crowded tables, his feet didn't track quite right, and the lights looked blurred. He bumped into the shoulders of gamblers at the tables and knocked a waiter off balance and ignored the angry curses.

Lew and Skin Deschamps and Tully were coming in from the street, red-faced and staggering and noisy, drunker than Ox.

Ox didn't give a damn what happened. He walked right into the three of them and jammed his elbow into Skin's chest and knocked Lew off balance with his shoulder. Lew slammed back into Tully and the two of them banged against the door frame. Skin was still off balance, and Ox grabbed his shoulder with his left hand and was winding up to slug him, when Lew flung his arms around his shoulders and yelled in his ear, "H'lo? Ox! Y' ol' bastard! C'mon! Belly up to the bar, we're celebratin'!"

Tully leaned on the wall, choking and gasping. Skin Deschamps twisted in Ox's grasp and Ox gripped with all his strength, with his thumb gouging under Skin's collar bone. Skin yelled hoarsely, and Lew hollered to the room in general, "Ever'body up t' th' bar! Ol' Lew's buyin'! Got myself engaged to the sweetes' li'l girl in th' whole God damn territory!"

Skin twisted free and crouched. The bowie knife was in his hand, his ferret face with spit on the beard snarling at Ox. Ox shoved Lew away, and Lew staggered back and brought up against the bar. Skin shuffled his feet and began to move in, but he was too drunk for the speed a knife fighter needed. Ox caught him with a short right between the eyes. Skin dropped to his knees and sprawled forward, face down. Ox pivoted as Tully pushed himself away from the wall and groped for his gun. Ox hit the side of Tully's jaw with a swinging left fist. Tully spun sideways and took two tottering steps and plunged across a poker table. Gamblers and chairs and cards went flying, and the bartender and three or four others were on Ox like a landslide, and bore him to the floor.

A dozen hands grabbed him and heaved him out onto the boardwalk. He got to his feet and fumbled for his Colt. The bartender stood in the doorway with a sawed-off shotgun, and a cluster of yammering faces behind him. He said, "Go on home! Sleep it off!"

Ox glared at him, and slowly wiped his mouth with his forearm. The bartender said, "Go on! Git!"

Ox turned and walked down the dark street, stumbling and muttering.

chapter twelve

Ox and Jake took the freight to Florence, and hardly spoke to each other the whole six days, coming and going. Jake seemed to be making a real effort to straighten out, and was never more than mildly drunk, although liquor was available at the stage stops. They brought back a load of pine timbers for a new warehouse for the Pioneer Flour Mill and delivered it before they drove in, late at night, to the livery barn.

Ox and Carlson sat in the office while Jake unhitched the team. Carlson got a bottle from a locked desk drawer and poured two drinks, and Jake came in and eyed the bottle, and Carlson poured him a stiff shot. Jake downed it without a shudder and said, "Thanks, Ed," and stood around fidgeting, while Ox told Carlson about the trip, and how Lew Barnes' coach had passed them twice, once on the way to Florence and once on the way back, and both times had cut in so close to the leaders his wheels had thrown gravel into their faces. Skin Deschamps, riding shotgun for Lew, had snarled at Ox, and Lew had laughed.

Carlson said, "I heard you punched Skin's head, over in the Hole in the Wall."

"I was loaded," Ox said, "or I guess I wouldn't have. I got Tully, too. Nailed 'em both good."

Carlson paid Jake, and Jake scuttled out.

"I'd keep an eye on 'em," Carlson said. "Your Injun kid was here while you were gone."

"Here! What for!"

"Well, I came in after lunch," Carlson said, "le's see, that was Tuesday, an' he was in the barn an' Chucho was tryin' to get him to go back to Mansfield's. Chucho says he doesn't like livin' in a house, wants to go with you on the wagons. Gwen came an' got him, figured he'd come here."

"The little fool," Ox said. "I better have a talk with him. Any hauling in sight?"

"Well, Etchells still hasn't got that steel from Yuma. If we could find a load for Yuma we could have the job. Trouble is, most everything comes *from* Yuma. Not much movin' that direction."

"I'll see what I can stir up, Ed. I want to talk to Mansfield about Flaco in the morning. See if Otero's back from Mexico."

In the morning, for the first time Ox didn't look forward to visiting the Pioneer News Depot. If he hadn't blurted out his suspicion of Lew, if he'd used a little tact and maybe hinted around without coming right out with it—but he still had no idea how he might have done it.

When he went in, Gwen was stocking shelves with stationery. Ox said, "Good morning, Gwen," but her back was turned, and she didn't answer. He went into the back room and found Mansfield working on his books.

Mansfield said, "Morning, Ox," and stuck the pen in a glass full of bird shot and leaned back in his swivel chair. "I hoped you'd come in. Our plan for the boy isn't working out.

He can't take civilization, I guess. Ran away the other afternoon. Ed Carlson said he was looking for you."

"He told me," Ox said. "Is Otero still gone?"

"Not back yet," Mansfield said. "Do you know a couple of buffalo hunters, Tully and . . . yes, you said Tully made some kind of trouble at Chucho Huerta's place." Mansfield called, "Gwen! Come in here, will you? Tell Ox what happened."

Gwen came in. She spoke stiffly, not looking at Ox. "The day after Flaco ran away, I talked to him about his hair. He finally agreed to have it cut. I took time off the next afternoon, and we were on our way to Greek Alex's barber shop. These men came out of a saloon and followed us, and several others joined them. They were laughing and making horrible jokes about Apaches and scalping. They made threats about you, too."

"You said they threatened you, too, didn't you, Gwen?" Mansfield asked. "For being friendly with the boy and Ox?"

"Yes," Gwen said. "The tall one took Flaco by the hair and flourished a knife and said he was going to c . . . collect his hair. And Flaco tried to get his knife he carries, and I held onto his arm, and the man said if I wasn't Lew's girl, he'd fix me, too, and that anyone who was friends with a dirty Apache was his enemy. And then Lew came out of the saloon. He slapped Tully's face and made them go away. Lew and I took Flaco home."

Ox suppressed the rage that was starting to boil in him. He said, "Don't you worry any more," and turned to leave.

"What are you going to do?" Gwen asked. "Ben, don't . . ." and Mansfield interrupted: "I talked to Owen Mason. He said Gwen should have had better sense than to be on Congress Street alone. Said he'd talk to Deschamps and Tully, but that we were all asking for trouble by keeping the boy around."

"Well, *I'll* talk to 'em!" Ox said. As he went out, Gwen ran after him and caught his arm and said, "Ben, you won't . . . *Please*, Ben!"

He pulled away from her and started his search. He found Lew Barnes at the Butterfield station, just in from a trip to Florence, but Skin Deschamps had already gone. Lew grinned at him and said, "Looks like you're on the prod. What's chewin' on you? That fracas in the Hole in the Wall? Hell, you started it, Ox. And everybody was drunk, anyway. Skin doesn't fool around. You better hope you don't find him."

"I'll find him," Ox said. "And if you mix in, I'll break your head."

Lew's face went still and his eyes slitted. He said, "Ox, boy, you and me are gonna tangle one of these days."

"So start tangling, you son of a bitch!" Ox said.

Lew gave him a long stare and said, "I know what's biting you, it's Gwen. So I guess I pass. But if you force it, you won't walk away from it." He went into the station.

Ox learned from Chucho Huerta where Deschamps and Tully were staying—an abandoned adobe shack out behind the brewery—and went there first. The plank door was padlocked. Through the window bars he could see a bare, dirty room with a pile of dirty clothes and a wad of blankets on the earth floor and a greasy frying pan on the *brasero*. In back of the shack was a makeshift corral—old boards and crooked mesquite poles, a wooden tub with no water in it, a pile of hay, and fresh horse manure.

He went to search the saloons, but nobody had seen the two buffalo hunters. He had dinner, and went to his room and rested a while. If the two didn't show up at the Hole in the Wall later, he'd hunt for them again tomorrow. He might have let it all pass, and they could send Flaco to Archuleta and it would blow over. But they had threatened Gwen.

About nine, he headed for the Hole in the Wall, and Owen Mason stopped him on the corner of Pennington. Owen said, "They tell me you're lookin' for Deschamps an' Tully. Now you listen. You keep out of the Hole in the Wall. I'll be dropping in there. You stay out, hear?"

Ox said, "Sure, Owen," and walked around him.

He went into the Hole in the Wall and looked over the heads of the gamblers at the tables, and through the layered smoke, he saw Skin Deschamps and Tully and Lew Barnes at the corner table with two others. Several men saw him, and the clatter of chips and the talk subsided until the room was quiet. As Ox started for the table, Lew saw him and got up and came over to him. Lew was drunk. He flung an arm over Ox's shoulder and said, "Y're just th' man I wanna see. Len' me a hundred, will ya, Ox? I'm just hittin' a hot streak. Been losin' up to now."

Ox said, "You're too stupid to see what those two are doing to you. Raise you right out of every pot. You bet, and Skin raises and Tully raises him, and you stay or raise, until it gets too steep for you, and you drop out. Then one of them drops out, and the other takes the pot. Everybody in town knows it but you."

Skin Deschamps stood up behind the table, and said, "You mouthy bastard!" and pulled his bowie knife. Tully and Ox had their guns half drawn, and men were knocking over chairs and scrambling for cover. Lew Barnes was drunk enough so he didn't realize what was going on. He said, "All right, you tight bastard. Hey, Skin! You got my money, how's t' len' me fifty?"

In the silence, he staggered to the table and sat down and said, "How 'bout it, Skin? Whose deal?"

The bartender shoved his sawed-off shotgun across the bar and said, "Now, listen here!"

Ox ignored him and, with his hand gripping his half-drawn Colt, started to walk to the table, and the swinging doors flapped open.

Behind him Jake Harris said, "God damn, Ox, I been lookin' all over for you. Where you s'pose I found this little bastard?"

Ox looked over his shoulder. Jake was dragging Flaco across the floor by one arm. He said, "He run away again. Found him in a wagon over at th' livery. Oughta chain him up like a pet bear." Jake shoved Flaco toward Ox and walked to the bar, drunk enough to be unaware of the tension in the room and the shotgun in the bartender's hands. He bounced a silver dollar on the bar and said, "Put out the bottle, huh?"

Skin said, "*Well* now, lookee there! The big bastard's little punk! Now ain't that a pretty head o' hair!" Ox looked around at him hastily and jerked at his Colt, and behind him, Tully said, "Stand real still!"

Ox hadn't heard Tully move around behind him but he felt the muzzle of the gun in his ribs. The bartender said, *"You! Tully! Hold it!"* and Tully said, "Anybody moves, I plug this son of a bitch! You got any ideas, Skin?"

Ox started to move, and Tully said, "Git your hands up!"

Slowly, Ox lifted his hands. Flaco looked hastily at him and back at Skin Deschamps, who was shuffling around the table, his yellow, horse teeth showing in a grin in the greasy tangle of beard.

"Figure I'll carve him up a little an' let the big boy watch it," he said. "Solve th' God damn Injun problem in this town right now."

Suddenly Flaco's skinning knife was in his hand, and he

slid two catlike steps to meet Skin. Skin's eyes popped wide.
He stopped and studied the boy. Flaco took another noiseless
step, crouching with the knife loose in his hand like a duelist's
rapier. He said, "Big mouth, you. Big wind. I gonna cut you'
stummick, me."

Two things happened at once—Lew Barnes drew his gun
and lunged and slugged Flaco on the head, and Jake Harris
hit Tully on the back of the head with a brass cuspidor.

Ox heard the "clunk", and felt Tully slump against his
back. He whirled and got him by the collar with one hand
and by the left wrist with the other and swung him off his
feet and threw him at Skin Deschamps. Tully's limp body
cartwheeled into Skin and they crashed across the poker
table and upset it onto the other two gamblers.

Lew Barnes, flushed and snarling, bent over the prostrate
boy. He cocked the Colt, and Ox hit him. Ox felt the blow
himself, clear up to his shoulder. Lew seemed to come apart
as he flew backward, arms and legs flailing disjointedly. Ox
turned toward the poker table where Tully lay sprawled and
Skin and the other two were struggling clear of the wreck-
age.

Jake threw a chair, not at anyone in particular, just threw
it, and it smashed the overhead lamp. There were shouts and
curses and the trample of boot heels. A fan of light from the
two lamps on the backbar cut the gloom somewhat, but the
room was a seething jumble of moving, shadowy figures and
a babble of yells and curses. Something, a chair or a man,
crashed through a window. Someone fell against Ox's knees,
and he stumbled and hit out at a shadow and felt his fist
smash against flesh. Over the yelling and the crash of glass
and the racket of overturning furniture, came a hoarse
scream of agony.

Ox put his head down and rammed his way to the overturned table. The first face he felt was smooth. A man
tripped and fell against him, and he felt the scrape of wiry
whiskers against his face and, immediately, a streak of fire
ran across his ribs. He yelled and got a handful of beard in
his left hand, shoved the man against the wall and hit him in
the ribs. The man screamed and dropped his knife. Ox held
him against the wall and hit him again, a short, vicious hook
in the ribs. The man groaned and collapsed, and Ox kicked
him as he lay crumpled against the wall.

There was a struggle in the doorway and someone burst in

and fired three shots into the ceiling and yelled, *"That's enough! That's enough!"*

The movement and the noise stopped.

Owen Mason, with the smoking pistol in his hand, said, "Bring a light, Smitty!"

The bartender brought a lamp from the back bar and righted a table and set the lamp down.

Men got up and stood silent. Others crowded in from outside. Ox looked around for Tully, but Tully wasn't there. He walked over and gathered Flaco up from the floor. The boy's head was bloody. It flopped loosely as Ox shifted him in his arms.

Two men lifted a man from behind the smashed poker table. One of them said, "This one's done for." Jake Harris hung limp in their arms, his mouth open, his eyes staring, and his belly one red smear of blood.

Ox stared at him stupidly for a moment, then it hit him. That was *Jake!* Gray faced and slack mouthed and old and blood smeared . . . and dead. *Jake Harris!* Something went sick inside him.

He held Flaco's slack body in his right arm and closed his eyes for a moment. Slowly, he stooped and laid Flaco on the floor, and straightened up. Standing spread-legged and bloody, he pulled the Colt. That was Skin Deschamps there, lying crumpled at the bottom of the wall.

Owen Mason jammed the muzzle of his gun into Ox's kidneys. "Drop it!" he said. "Right now!"

Ox turned his head and stared at the deputy.

"Drop it!"

Ox shoved his Colt into the holster. He bent and gathered Flaco into his arms again. Lew Barnes raised his head and managed to prop himself on his elbows. Ox kicked him in the face. Lew's head thumped on the floor, and Ox stepped across him and started for the door.

Owen Mason stepped in front of him, his face ugly. He said, "You son of a bitch, I told you. You came in here anyway. I'm gonna . . . "

Ox kept on walking, and Owen didn't get out of his way, so Ox rammed into him with his shoulder. Owen staggered to one side, and Ox walked out.

He was a block up the street, with people running toward the saloon and bumping into him and hurrying on, before he could tell that Flaco was still breathing. Ox turned the corner and began to walk to the Army Hospital, up on Calle de la Guardia.

Someone called his name. He ignored it and went on. Then it came to him that it was Gwen calling, and her steps and someone else's running to overtake him. Gwen and Mansfield came up. Out of breath, Gwen said between gasps, *"Ben! Is he dead? Is Flaco dead?"*

"He's alive," Ox said. He kept on walking.

Mansfield said, "He ran away again. We were hunting for him. Someone told us you were carrying him along here, and . . ."

"Ben! You're bleeding!" Gwen's voice was high and scared.

"Yeah," Ox said. "Lew's friend Deschamps took a knife to me."

"Is he the one that hurt Flaco? He *said* he would."

"No," Ox said bitterly. "That was your husband-to-be. Clubbed him down with a gun. Would have shot him if I hadn't knocked him down."

"You're lying," Gwen said, trotting to keep up. "You're lying about Lew!"

"Am I? They killed Jake Harris. With a knife. Cut his belly open."

Gwen stopped. Her hands flew to her open mouth. "No! *Oh, no!*" She began to sob, and hurried to catch up. She was still crying when they reached the hospital.

They put five stitches in Flaco's scalp. The pain woke him up, but he just sat there like a wooden Indian and endured it.

The long slash across Ox's ribs was still bleeding. The surgeon said his ribs had deflected the thrust, or it would have killed him. They bandaged him around the waist, and the surgeon lent him a shirt too small to button around his thick, bandaged middle.

The surgeon wouldn't let Flaco stay in the hospital. He said he had no business treating Indians at all, and maybe he'd broken some regulation. Mansfield sent to Leatherwood's corral for a wagon with hay in the bed. When they put Flaco in, Gwen sat with him and held his hand. Ox sat on the seat, crowding Mansfield and the driver, as they went to Mansfield's house. Gwen wanted to accompany Ox to his room to be sure he was all right, but he refused curtly, and the driver took him home.

He couldn't find a position comfortable enough to let him sleep, so he sent the clerk for a pint of whiskey and drank half of it before he dropped off. Twice during the night, he awoke groaning, having rolled over and hurt himself.

Owen Mason was waiting for him when he came out of his room about nine in the morning. Mason started in bawling him out, but Ox broke in and demanded: "Who killed Jake?"

"I don't know," the deputy said.

"It was Deschamps," Ox said. "Where is he?"

"You don't know it was Deschamps," Mason said. "Tully carries a knife, too, and . . ."

"Where's Tully?" Ox asked.

"I don't know that either," Mason said. "Nobody saw him after the brawl. Anyway, some of the others had knives, and that God damn Apache kid had one. Somebody likely picked it up and used it on Jake."

"Why don't you lock those two up till you find out?" Ox asked.

"Listen, God damn it! Nobody knows what happened in the dark that way. Anyway, you started it, an' if I hadn't stopped you from killin' Skin, you'd be up for murder right now!"

"Who you been listenin' to, Owen? Skin went after Flaco with a knife. And Lew Barnes slugged him with his gun. What you want me to do, stand there and watch? Tully had a gun on me, that's why Jake hit him. You know that?"

"Well, I ain't arrestin' nobody," Mason said. "You keep away from them. Keep the hell out of the Hole in the Wall, and . . ."

"When I find 'em," Ox said, "just don't get in my way."

Mason had no sooner gone than Gwen came in. She said, "Ben, about Jake, I can't tell you how sorry I am. That poor, loyal little man! He loved you, didn't he?" She sat down on the bench beside him. "Ben, are *you* all right?" She put her hand on his arm. "Does it hurt a great deal?"

"I'm all right," Ox said.

"Mr. Mansfield's making arrangements for the service," she said. "He knows you'd want to take care of it, but with you hurt like this, he thought . . ."

"Tell him thanks for me," Ox said. "I appreciate it. I'll pay for it. How's Flaco?"

"Well, he seems to be all right. He won't stay in bed, and Concha's making a fuss over him. And Ben, I'm . . . well, I know it was Lew that hit him. Mr. Mansfield heard about it. He was drunk, Ben. He didn't know what he was doing."

"He's a liar and a thief, and maybe worse," Ox said bluntly. "Real happy marriage you're going to have."

She got up from the bench. Her face was white as she picked up her bag and walked out.

Ox's side was on fire. He checked the loads in the Colt and holstered it, and walked bent over, the six long blocks to Carlson's Livery Stable. Men spoke to him, but he ignored them, and watched the alleys and the saloon doors. He didn't think Skin Deschamps would be up and around this morning, not after those two punches in the short ribs, but Tully had got out of the Hole in the Wall before Owen Mason stopped the brawl, and Tully would favor a shot in the back. The two of them were going to answer for Jake—but not today. Not till he could straighten up and move freely, unless he ran into them face to face.

In the office, Carlson looked at him quizzically, and got the bottle out of the desk drawer. "Well," he said, "I hear the town's full of busted heads and sprung backs."

"Jake's dead," Ox said. "I have to see Mansfield about the funeral."

"Yeah, I heard," Carlson said. He poured whisky into two tin cups and handed one to Ox. Ox forgot, and reached with his left hand, and almost dropped the cup. It felt as if a red hot spike had driven into his ribs. Carlson went on: "An' Lew Barnes's got a jaw like a cantaloupe, an' Skin Deschamps got four busted ribs, and Tully a lump on the back of his head. How bad is yours?"

"Skin cut me across the ribs," Ox said. "I'll be all right in a few days."

"Listen, Ox, nothin' would've happened if it wasn't for that damn kid," Carlson said. "An' now everybody's beat up an' cut up, an' Jake's killed, an' you'll have two men gunnin' for you, an' maybe three, if Lew Barnes is sore enough."

"Soon as Flaco's head's healed up, I'll take him to Archuleta," Ox said. "Quit yammering about him."

"If you'd've done that before ... but no, you get your neck bowed. Nobody's gonna pound any sense into Ox Davis! You been around mules too long. You're gettin' just like 'em."

Ox got up and walked out. He had breakfast at a Mexican cafe on India Triste so he wouldn't have to face the questions and the funny remarks in the Maison Doree, and went to the Pioneer News Depot.

Gwen seemed not to know whether she was mad at him or

sorry for him. Probably both. Mansfield told him about the
funeral arrangements, and Ox asked him to order flowers
from Carrillo's Gardens, and the black hearse with the
matched black team. Ox went to the Methodist Episcopal
manse and made arrangements with the preacher. If a
preacher and a Bible might give Jake a better sendoff to
wherever he was going, well, he'd have them.

They buried Jake that evening. Ox heard little of the
perfunctory service. He was remembering all the times he'd
dumped Jake into a horse trough, and lent him money and
got sore at him; and remembered, too, that Jake had never
really let him down, not once—stumbling drunk, or sick with
the shakes, he'd always come through when Ox really needed
him—that time he cooled off Lew Barnes and his shotgun
messenger when Lew ran over the harness, and times when
they'd been stuck in a bad river ford, or gear broke down, or
a vicious mule had to be shod; that night he'd sat out there
by himself, watching the mules and the wagons when Ox
took Gwen and Ostrander in to Ehrenberg—and last night.
Last night, when he'd come charging into that brawl like a
bear gone berserk, and had taken a knife in his guts. Ox
didn't have any illusions as to why he'd done it—it was for
Ox Davis, not Jake Harris.

Beside Ox, Gwen was crying silently. She didn't say anything, but held onto his arm. Ed Carlson had brought them in
his surrey. When it was over, they took Gwen and Mansfield
home. There was no one else.

Ox and Carlson had a drink or two at Abadie's and dinner
at the Maison Doree, and drove back to the livery. Lieutenant Armstrong from the Quartermaster's office was waiting for them.

The lieutenant said, "Well, Davis, I hear you fought a
major engagement last night. They brought that buffalo
hunter to the Army Hospital with four broken ribs."

"You just stop by to gossip?" Ox asked.

"No. We have a load of freight for Camp Apache, and no
army equipment available." He turned to Carlson. "Can you
handle it?"

"Ox can't drive," Carlson said. "He's cut up."

"Chucho can drive," Ox said. "He's a good man. I can
haul on a brake. I'll swamp for Chucho."

"You think you ought to?" Carlson asked. "You're in no
shape to fight, if them Apaches . . . that Juan Pedro's still on

the loose. Be a good thing if you got outa town a while, though."

"We'll furnish an escort," Lieutenant Armstrong said. "Anyway, they've got Juan Pedro on the run. He's only got about ten men left, and their horses are giving out."

"You gonna send that Corporal Cooper?" Ox asked.

Armstrong laughed. "Hell, no! He's a good non-com. We want to keep him in one piece."

Next morning, as Chucho Huerta drove the rig to the Quartermaster's Corral to load up, he turned in Lilly's saddle and said to Ox, who was in the lead wagon, "You think I can handle it, Mr. Ox? I don' know. I'm never drive big team, only 'roun' town, w'en we gotta take wagon to load somewhere."

"You'll do fine," Ox said. "All you gotta do is jerk the line and swing the blacksnake. Anything comes up, I'll tell you what to do."

They loaded twelve tons of freight—kegs of horseshoes, picks and shovels, a dozen new McClellan saddles, rope and chain, and cases of Springfield ammunition. Sergeant Finlay was ready with twelve troopers.

Ox was glad to be going. Camp Apache was 230 miles of rough road way up in the foothills of the White Mountains. Eleven or twelve days each way, with luck and no breakdowns. If he was careful, his cut would heal, and he wouldn't be running into Tully or Skin Deschamps or Lew Barnes. He wasn't ready for that, yet. And these days, although the thought of Gwen—a frustration and a misery and an ache in his heart—was never out of his mind, he didn't want to see her, not while she still thought Lew Barnes was just a happy-go-lucky boy who would settle down when she married him.

For the start of the trip, Ox rode in the lead wagon, sitting up on a crate with his head brushing the bowed canvas top, where he could holler at the mules and help Chucho with the cussing. Sergeant Finlay's escort led the way into the turn onto Main Street, yelling at the traffic to make room for the mules to swing. As they rolled north out of town, Lew Barnes passed them on his run to Florence. Another shotgun messenger sat in Skin Deschamps' place. Lew stared straight ahead. His swollen jaw was tied in a white bandage.

chapter thirteen

The eleven-day haul, ending twelve thousand feet up in the White Mountains, was without incident. They delivered the supplies to Captain Andrews, for the 205 enlisted men and eight officers of Companies E and D of the 6th Cavalry and E and C of the 8th Infantry, and Company A of the Indian Scouts, who were out chasing Juan Pedro and his eight or ten surviving warriors north from the border.

They made the return trip in nine days, and by the time Chucho pushed the team back into the traffic of Main Street, Tucson, Ox's side had almost healed. He watched the people on the boardwalks, but didn't see Gwen or Lew Barnes, or Skin Deschamps or Tully. He was relieved. Maybe, after he sent Flaco to Archuleta, or Otero took the boy to Mexico, he could choose his own time and place to remind Skin and Tully about Jake Harris.

Carlson wasn't in the office, and Ox watched the hostlers unhitch. Twenty mules raised the dust of the corral, rolling the sweat and harness itch out of their tough hides. It was time for dinner when Carlson came in.

"How'd it go?" he asked. "Any trouble? Fight off any 'Paches?"

"Not a sign of 'em," Ox said. "Ed, Chucho's gonna make a skinner. Maybe we oughta think about another team and some new wagons."

"It's worth thinkin' about, Ox. You're pilin' up some capital. We could go fifty-fifty." Carlson poured drinks, and leaned back with his chair tilted against the desk. He said, "I saw Miss Goodfield the other day."

Ox's heart gave a bump in his chest. He hadn't wanted to ask, but he was anxious to hear about her. "How is she?" he asked. "Any more trouble? How's Flaco?"

"She said his head's mended pretty good, but he sticks close to home. Skin Deschamps started ridin' shotgun for

110

Barnes again, just yesterday. Too bad you didn't bust his back for him."

"What about Tully?" Ox asked.

"Haven't seen him. Nobody else has, far as I know."

They had a couple of drinks in Abadie's, and went to dinner at the Maison Doree. As they got up to leave, Carlson said, "Oh, yeah. That U.S. Marshal and Ogden, the Pinkerton man, came around to see you. Wanted to talk to you."

"What about?"

"Well, nothin' much, seemed to me. They got a lot of suspicions but no evidence. Seemed like they just wanted to see if you remembered anything you hadn't told 'em about the time the girl's father got killed, or maybe whether Lew Barnes had ever let anything slip when he was drunk."

"I'll go see 'em tomorrow. Where they staying?"

"They're at the Palace. I think they set up a kind of office in the jail. They're in and out of town, nosin' around."

Ox said, "I'll see Gwen in the morning, Ed. If Flaco's head's all right, we're going to send him down to Archuleta. How do you get in touch with him?"

"I write to a fellow in Nogales and he takes it out to Archuleta," Carlson said.

Ox's wound was still tender to the touch, but it no longer kept him awake. He slept that night as though he had been sandbagged.

He wasn't eager to see Gwen, but he couldn't stand not to, and the need to discuss Flaco provided the excuse. When he went to the book store in midmorning, she was working at the desk behind the counter. The constraint was still there— the level glance with no warmth, the beautiful face with no expression on it.

She talked to him freely enough, but she was all business: "The sooner we can send Flaco away, the better. He's well enough to travel. You ought to go, too, and not come back."

"Me!" Ox said. "Why me?" It hurt him that she could advise this so coldly.

"That awful man has threatened you and Flaco, too. He apparently doesn't care who knows it. Even Lew has threatened you. He lost two teeth. Did you know that? You have a great talent for making enemies."

"Including you, I guess," Ox said. And for the first time, there was a crack in the ice. Gwen looked hastily away from him and got a handkerchief from her pocket and dabbed at her eyes.

"No, Ben. Not your enemy. Not ever. I ... I just wish ... Lew isn't bad. He's a good man, Ben."

"What about how he hit Flaco with his gun?" Ben asked, and was immediately sorry. This had hit home, and he didn't want to hurt Gwen, not any way at all.

When she faced him again, there were tears in her eyes. She said, "He ... he said Flaco had a knife. He was afraid Deschamps would kill him ... would kill Flaco. And he said you stood there and did nothing."

"Gwen, didn't he tell you Tully had a gun in my back? If Jake hadn't knocked him down, he'd likely have shot me. And Jake got killed for it. Fighting for me."

She was crying now, and not doing anything about it, just sitting there with her hands in her lap and letting the tears run.

"I ... I don't know what to think," she said. "I don't know what the truth is. Lew wouldn't lie to me. But I don't think you would, either. Would you, Ben? Would you?"

Ox said, "If he had to hit somebody to stop a killing, why didn't he hit Skin? It was Skin that pulled a knife and made the threats. Why didn't Lew stop *him*?"

She put both hands to her face and said, "I don't *know*! I don't *know*! He still says Flaco is Apache, and they all hate Apaches so, as if that made killing all right."

Ox reached out and laid his hand on her head. He swallowed painfully, and had to try twice before his voice worked right: "Gwen, won't you listen? I ... I ... ." But he couldn't do it—couldn't tell her he loved her, and that even if she never looked at him, he couldn't stand to think of her married to that son of a bitch!

Gwen stood up and blew her nose. She smiled at him, a sad kind of smile and said, "Ben, I know. I've known for a long time, and I hate all the bitter words. And if you do ... well if you do love me ... That's what you meant, isn't it?"

A thousand words, a thousand avowals crowded in his mind, trying to get themselves said, and all he could do was swallow again and nod his head and look out the window.

Gwen blew her nose again, and said, briskly, "Come to the house tonight, Ben. I'm supposed to go to dinner with Lew, he'll be back from Florence, but I'll leave word for him at the depot. We can talk with Mr. Mansfield, and make plans for Flaco."

"Ed Carlson will write to Archuleta when we're ready to send Flaco," Ox said. "I'll be there about eight."

He started to leave, and she came around the counter and took his hand. "Ben, we're friends again, aren't we?" She looked up into his eyes.

He managed to smile. "Yes," he said. "I never thought any different."

As it turned out, he didn't get to Mansfield's until much later. He had dinner and was coming out of the Cosmopolitan Hotel about quarter to eight, when he heard the Florence stage coming down Main Street at a gallop. He stopped in the hotel doorway to watch it go by.

Somebody yelled and pointed and pedestrians began to run after the coach. As it swept by, Ox saw Skin Deschamps driving and, beside him, Lew Barnes looking green and gripping a bloody bandage on his left forearm. The coach skidded on the turn into Pennington Street, and Ox heard the brakes screech as it slid to a stop in front of the Butterfield station. He ran after it.

There was already a small crowd when he got there. Skin was helping Lew down over the wheel, and the manager was yelling at them. Ox shoved his way through.

The manager was purple in the face, shouting, "Not *another* one! Where the hell, *this* time?"

"Point of Mountain Station, a mile or two this side, like the time they stuck up Lew and Billy Mayo," Skin said.

Somebody shoved Ox roughly with an elbow, and he turned and saw Benson, the U.S. Deputy Marshal. The manager saw Benson forcing his way through, and said, "*Another* one, Benson! Over nine hundred in the box, and bank drafts and checks!"

"That right, Skin?" the marshal asked. "They get the money again?"

Skin let go of Lew, who leaned on the wheel, white faced, holding his bandaged arm. Ox saw the gap in his lower teeth.

"Yeah, they got it," Skin said, staring at the marshal as though daring him to comment. "But I got one of 'em. Back in the boot."

"Show me," the marshal said. He roared at the crowd, "*Stand back, there!*"

Owen Mason rode up and handed his reins to somebody and began to push the people back. He pushed Ox, and Ox shoved him out of the way and went to the rear of the coach with Skin and the marshal and the manager. The boot cover wasn't buckled, and Skin reached in and braced himself and pulled, and a dead man fell like a sack of wet meal onto the ground. Skin rolled him face up with his foot.

Tully lay staring at the sky, his open eyes filmed with dust, his cheekbones and forehead pitted with small, blue holes, one edge of his beaded vest ragged, and his chest bloody.

Benson said, "Friend of yours, ain't he?"

"I used t' think so," Deschamps said.

"Who else saw it?" the marshal asked. "Where's the passengers?"

Lew Barnes had managed to get to the back of the coach. "Wasn't any," he said. "Two miners got off at Point of Mountain. That's all we had. Tully and two others rode out of some rocks and stopped us. Skin reached for his scatter-gun, and Tully cut loose with a six gun. Got me in the arm. Skin got him. Both barrels."

"What about the other two?" the marshal asked.

"Hell, they had us dead to rights," Skin said. "My Greener empty an' Lew shot. I threw down the box an' they got it an' rode off."

"An' didn't cut you down. An' no witnesses," the marshal said.

"That's right," Lew said. "Only Tully, here. I figure he's pretty good evidence."

"You figure you need evidence?" Benson asked.

Skin bristled like a fighting cock. "What th' hell you think you're gettin' at?"

The manager said, wearily, "Somebody get a doctor for Lew. We'll get the facts down for my report. Pinkertons aren't going to like this."

Benson said, "No. That can wait. I got some questions."

"*Questions!*" Skin said. "God damn it, we just told you!"

"I got questions," Benson said. "And you'll answer! Over at the jail." He swung around and looked for Owen Mason and said, "Mason, get rid of the body, will you, whatever you do with 'em? And bring all his stuff to the jail. His clothes, what's in his pockets, everything. And send a doctor."

"I'll take care of it," Mason said.

Lew Barnes's face was gray with pain. He said, "What the hell *is* this! I get stood up and shot, and you take *me* to jail! Why aren't you getting up a posse? Are we under arrest?"

"Maybe an' maybe not," the marshal said. "Just come on, now."

"God damn it, I'm *shot!*" Lew shouted.

"You made it twenty miles, you can make it a few

blocks," the marshal said. "Mason'll send a doctor an' somebody'll loan you a horse." He took Lew by the arm, and said
to the deputy, "Mason, get out there right away after you
bring me Tully's stuff. Don't let anybody mess around, I'll
want a look at those tracks."

Benson swung around to Skin Deschamps, who was staring
at him hard-eyed. He said, "Well, you comin', or am I gonna
take you?"

Skin looked at the crowd and made an elaborate shrug,
shoulders hunched and palms spread. As he turned to follow
the marshal, he bumped into Ox. He jammed his elbow into
Ox's sore ribs and snarled, "Git outa people's way, you . . . "

Before he could say it, Ox grabbed his face with his right
hand and shoved hard, with his weight behind it. Skin staggered back with his arms flung out in a vain attempt to keep
his balance, and sat down hard at the marshal's feet. His gun
bounced out of the holster. He reached for it, and Marshal
Benson stepped on his wrist.

The marshal said, "Funny them road agents left you your
gun. Feller'd think you might get 'em in the back when they
rode off with the box." He took his foot off Skin's wrist and
picked up the Colt and shoved it under his belt.

Skin got up, rubbing his wrist. He said, "They told us to
throw 'em down, an' we did. They left 'em lay, an' we got
'em, after."

Somebody led a horse through the crowd and, as Lew
mounted awkwardly, grimacing with pain, Marshal Benson
plucked Lew's fancy gun from the holster and stuck that one
in his belt, too. He said to the crowd, "Now you folks go on
about your business," and seeming to see Ox for the first
time, said, "Davis, come see me in the mornin', will you? At
the jail. Bring the girl, huh?"

Ox walked to Mansfield's house. When Gwen saw his face,
she knew something had happened. Ox had thought he'd get
a lot of satisfaction out of telling her that Lew was under
suspicion of engineering another holdup of himself, but somehow, now, he was reluctant to do so. He didn't want to be
the one to pile trouble on her. He waited until they were
seated in the living room, and Mr. and Mrs. Mansfield came
in.

Mansfield said, "You're a little late, Ox. Well, I guess it
doesn't matter. Now . . ."

Ox looked down at his boots. He said, "Little excitement

over at the Butterfield station. Deschamps and Lew were held up."

Nobody said anything. Gwen stared at him, her eyes showing the horror he had known would be there. Mrs. Mansfield got up hastily and put an arm around Gwen's shoulders.

Mansfield said, "Lew seems to be a favorite target."

"He got shot," Ox said, and Gwen exclaimed something he didn't catch. He hastened to say, "Not bad. Just in the arm. He's over at the jail, him and Deschamps."

Gwen got up, "I'm going over there."

Ox said, "The marshal wants to ask 'em some questions. I don't think he'd let you in, not right now."

Slowly she sat down again. "But if he's *hurt* . . . why do they . . . ?"

"It isn't bad," Ox insisted. "They sent for a doctor. The marshall has to get the facts as soon as he can."

She sat staring at nothing, and Ox said, "They killed Tully."

"Tully!" Mansfield exclaimed. "You mean he was with them?"

"Well, not exactly," Ox said. "Seems he's the one stuck up the stage, him and two others, they said, and Skin got him with a shotgun. They brought him in."

"Why, he's their friend, their partner, isn't he?" Mansfield said. "Why would he . . . ?"

"You've got me," Ox said. "That's the way they told it."

"Well, I guess that clears Lew and Deschamps," Mansfield said.

Gwen came out of her trance. "Of course! Of course it does!" she said.

Ox conquered the urge to tell her what he thought. He said, "Gwen, he'll be all right. You can see him tomorrow. And the marshal said to bring you there, he wants to see us both."

"Us? You and me? What can we tell him?"

"I don't know, Gwen. Only that's what he told me. Now, about Flaco . . ."

But she wasn't listening, just looking at him and not seeing him. Mrs. Mansfield said, "Not tonight, Ben. There's no hurry now, is there? I mean, wasn't that Tully the one that threatened Flaco? And if he's . . . he's . . ."

"He wasn't the only one," Ox said. "Skin Deschamps, too. I think we should get Flaco out of here as soon as we can."

Mrs. Mansfield pulled gently at Gwen's arm. "Come on, dear. You can see Lew tomorrow. Come to bed now. I'm sure he's all right."

"Ox is right," Mansfield said. "As far as Flaco's concerned this doesn't change things. But we'll talk about it tomorrow."

Gwen left the room with Mrs. Mansfield's arm around her. Mansfield went to the door with Ox. He said, "Do you think this takes the suspicion off Barnes? I mean about the last one, too? There's been a lot of talk."

"I think he thought it would," Ox said. "Him and Skin."

"You think they'd murder their own friend to . . . to . . ."

"Hell yes, I think so," Ox said. "Benson does too."

"Well," Mansfield said, "Gwen's pretty shaken up. When does Benson want to see her?"

"Tell her I'll be around at ten o'clock," Ox said.

When he called for Gwen in the morning, she insisted on going around to Lew's place first, the two-room adobe house he had rented on India Alegre. The door was padlocked and the shutters closed.

Ogden, the Pinkerton man, was at the jail with Benson. He placed a chair at the table for Gwen. She asked Benson, "Where have you got Lew? Is he in jail?"

"You think I should have held him, Miss?" Benson asked. "If you know anything, you better tell me."

"Why did you bring him here if you didn't have anything against him?" she demanded. "Even before he saw a doctor. I must say . . ."

"Miss," Benson interrupted, "he ain't hurt. Just a nick on the arm. Doc Wilbur fixed him up, right here. All I did was question him an' Skin. Had to get the facts, didn't I? Believe me, if I had any more than a hunch, they'd be in a cell right now!"

"Well, then, why aren't you after the robbers?"

"Don't try to tell me my job, Miss! Owen Mason's out there now, an' Ogden an' me are goin' out as soon as you answer some questions."

"I've told you I don't know anything about who killed my father," Gwen said. "How could I know anything about last night?"

Benson asked, "Was Lew an' them two in Ehrenberg when Ox brought you an' Ostrander in, after the shootin'?"

"Why, yes," Gwen said. "At least, Lew was. He got a room for me. He was very good to me."

Ox said, "I didn't see Skin and Tully that night, but I went right back to the wagons. They were there the next day, anyway."

"Want you to look at something, Miss," Benson said. "Something you might've seen up there by Desert Well an' maybe forgot you saw." He turned in the swivel chair and reached into a cabinet against the wall, and brought out a black sombrero and shotgun chaps and a bloody shirt. He put them on the table, and got a torn, bloody, beaded vest out of the cabinet, and said, "Miss, you ever see this before?"

Gwen shuddered and looked away and back again. She said, "It's Tully's, isn't it? Yes, I saw it that day he and Deschamps stopped me, the day I was taking Flaco to the barber."

"How about up by Desert Well, when those fellers shot up the coach?"

"I didn't see anything," Gwen said. "I've told you. We were all inside, with the curtains closed."

"Well, all right, Miss. We kind of hoped . . . "

Suddenly, looking at the vest, Ox thought, by God, I can prove it! Got the son of a bitch! And maybe Lew and Skin, too! He said, "Let me see that," and Benson handed it to him. Ox had remembered turning that corner with the team up in Prescott, the first time he'd seen Gwen and her father and later, in the station dining room at Desert Well, her father's derby hat, the elegant coat, the flowered vest—and the ornate watch chain stretching from vest pocket to vest pocket. A heavy watch chain dangled from a pocket of Tully's Indian vest. He could have been just stupid enough . . .

He laid the vest across his knees and picked up the end of the chain. "Was this your father's?"

She made a grimace of disgust at the blood on the vest, and took the chain. "No," she said. "No, I'm sure it isn't."

She pulled the heavy gold watch from the pocket. A double-O buckshot had gone through it. "No," she said. "I know this wasn't his."

Ox's fierce elation died.

Benson said, "Well, all right, Miss, I guess that's all," and Ox and Gwen stood up.

The Pinkerton man said, "Have you seen Barnes, Miss Goodfield? Did he tell you they fired him and Deschamps?"

Gwen whirled around. *"What?"*

"The Butterfield manager told us, Miss Goodfield."

"Without one bit of evidence," Gwen said softly. "After he got shot defending Butterfield property." She got up and walked out.

Ox took her home. At the door, she asked him if he saw Lew to tell him she wanted to see him.

As Ox turned down Ochoa Street on his way to Carlson's, he saw Barnes and Deschamps riding out of Smith's Corral. Lew had his left arm in a sling. He was mounted on a well-put-up Morgan, with a new saddle and saddlebags, and had a carbine in the saddle boot. Skin Deschamps rode the uncurried pinto with one blue eye that Ox had seen many times at the hitchrack in front of the Hole in the Wall.

They pulled up when they saw him. Skin sat hunched sideways—the ribs Ox had smashed must still be bothering him. Neither of them spoke as Ox crossed the street to them.

Ox said, "Gwen wants to see you, Lew."

"I'll see her when I'm ready," Lew said.

"See *you* when we're ready, too," Skin said.

"I'm ready," Ox said, and put his hand on the Colt.

Lew jammed spurs into the Morgan, and it squealed and pitched and broke into a gallop. Skin lifted his glass-eyed pinto into a trot and went after Lew.

Ox thought, I wonder if they've got the wind up. Maybe they're pulling out.

Hal Smith came out of the gate and said, "Howdy, Ox. That Barnes knows good horseflesh."

"He buy the Morgan?" Ox asked.

"I think he will. He wants to try it out. Never had no use for a horse, but now Butterfield fired him, he needs one. He'll keep it here if he buys it."

Two blocks down the street, Lew slid the Morgan on its rump and got off and tied it in front of the Hole in the Wall. Skin got down and followed Lew inside. Suddenly Ox realized that if Skin left town, he might never catch up with him. He went after them.

He hadn't noticed Owen Mason leaning on the wall outside, behind the horses at the rack. As he turned toward the door, Mason said, "You keep out of there."

"Who says?" Ox said. "You let Barnes and Skin go in."

"That's just it. I don't want no more trouble. For God sake, let it ride, will you?"

Ox decided he couldn't buck Skin and Lew and Mason,

and the bartender, too. He turned away, then swung back. "What'd you find out at Point of Mountain?"

"Nothin'. Just a lot of horse tracks, and blood on the ground where Skin dropped Tully. Looked like they said, Tully an' two or three more. Benson an' Ogden are on their way out there, now."

chapter fourteen

When Ox went to the livery office in the morning, Mansfield was there talking to Carlson. As Ox came in, Mansfield said, "We're talking about Flaco, Ox. I thought we better send him south right away. Skin's hanging around town with Lew. He hates the boy, and he might take it out on him, just to get back at you. Ed here says he'll write to Archuleta."

"How long will it take, Ed?" Ox asked.

"Well, I'll send it on the stage today. Oughta get an answer day after tomorrow, if my letter gets to Archuleta right away."

Carlson wrote the letter, and Ox took it to the Butterfield station, where the stage for Nogales was about to pull out.

In the afternoon, he went to the jail. Ogden was there, and Ox asked him what they'd found at the scene of the hold-up.

Ogden said, "Nothing but a lot of horse tracks. Where Tully's horse ran off, and two others rode up to the ambush with him, and rode away again. Benson said the tracks were all made by one horse. Said it was a paddler, throws its front feet out sideways and you could tell. He thinks they rigged it together, the three of them, and then Skin killed Tully to get them off the hook, and rode Tully's horse back and forth to make it look like several riders."

"Benson's sure?" Ox asked.

"No, he's not sure, but that's what he hopes to prove. They told him they figured they'd do some prospecting, now they've got no job."

"Couldn't Benson jail 'em on some charge?" Ox asked. "Keep 'em salted away while he investigates?"

"Like what?" Ogden asked. "There's no evidence to hold 'em on."

"Well, how about that scalp hunting business?" Ox asked. "I've heard Skin bragging about it. And Jake and I found a whole Mexican family scalped, down by Calabasas."

"If he's killing Mexicans, we could hold him. But if he's selling Apache scalps, why there's no law."

Ox saw Herm Welisch in the afternoon, and arranged to take a load of staples and olives and oranges up to Florence. Herm was expecting the delivery, up from Sonora, and Ox could leave Saturday afternoon. Welisch said he would arrange for a load for the return trip.

Thursday afternoon, Ox and Carlson were coming out of Abadie's, and Lew Barnes and Skin Deschamps rode by. They had slickers and bed rolls behind their cantles, and Skin was leading a pack mule, with a pick and shovel under the ropes of the squaw hitch that held the pack.

At four-thirty, Friday, Ox met the stage from Nogales. The driver had a message from Archuleta, who would meet the Saturday stage at the side road to his place.

Ox went to the Pioneer News Depot. Gwen greeted him noncommitally. He told her everything was ready for Flaco to go. She smiled then, and said, "I'm going to miss the little monkey. He drives Concha frantic, but she mothers him and overfeeds him. He's actually put on weight."

Mansfield came in from the back room. "Ever since we told him he's going to Archuleta, we've almost had to sit on him. What time's the stage, Ox?"

"Eight A.M.," Ox said. "I'll come around for him."

"We'll have him ready," Mansfield said, and went back into the room.

Gwen went on working as though she were alone. Ox coughed, and said, "Did Lew come to see you?"

"Yes," she said.

He waited, but she went on scratching with her pen on some bills, and Ox said, "I hear he's prospecting."

"He is," she said. "In the Aztec Mining District, down in the Santa Ritas. Not prospecting, actually. He and Mr. Deschamps bought a good claim from a Mexican."

"How's he know it's good?" Ox asked. "He ever do any mining?"

"Mr. Deschamps looked it over," Gwen said. "He knows what he's doing."

"So he and Lew are partners," Ox said. "Must make you feel good, Lew teamed up with a fine man like that."

Gwen flushed but didn't drop her gaze. She said, "Does it concern you?"

"You bet it does!" he said, and walked out.

Ox went to Mansfield's at seven-thirty Saturday morning, shaven and shining, with his hair trimmed and boots polished. When Gwen brought Flaco out, Ox wondered who had tied him down and curried him. His clothing was clean, his face was clean except for a smear of fried egg on his mouth, even his long hair was combed. If only he wouldn't wear that Indian style flat-brimmed sombrero with the tall, undented crown! Looked like he *belonged* on a reservation!

Gwen was smiling. "He's as hard to hold as an unbroken colt!" she said.

"You coming, too?" Ox asked.

"Oh, yes," she said. "He insisted. I think I've made a conquest."

Flaco suddenly remembered. He grabbed Ox's hand and shook it solemnly, and said, "Howdydo. Pleesta meetcha."

"Part of his new social graces," Gwen said. "We've been having lessons in deportment."

"We go," Flaco said. "*Vamos*, eh?"

"Well, no sadness of farewell, anyway," Ox said. "Come on."

There were a lot of passengers for Nogales, too many for one coach, and a hostler was hitching a team to an extra one. Ox left Gwen and Flaco by the door, and went in and bought Flaco's ticket. The first coach was full. Men were staring at Flaco from the station platform and the coach windows. One of them said, "Don't try puttin' that bastard Apache in here!"

Ox led Flaco to the second coach. There was a passenger already inside, and Ox said, "If you object to riding with a Mexican boy, get out!"

The man gaped at him, and looked away, staring out the far window, and a passenger got out of the full coach and walked back to Ox. He was Mexican, and he looked as tough as Archuleta. There was a huge cap-and-ball revolver stuck under the waistband of his pants. He aimed a thumb at Flaco and asked, "He's Mexican? He ain't Apache?"

"He's Mexican," Ox said.

The Mexican smiled at Flaco and took his arm, and said, "*Subes tu, chamaco!* Get in. We ride to Nogales together, eh?"

Gwen stood waving as Flaco's coach pulled out in the wake of the other, then turned and walked away. Ox overtook her. Her face was sad as she said, "They all hate him so! Poor little boy!"

On the way to the book shop, all she said was, "I hope Mr. Otero will find a good home for him."

"He'll be all right, now," Ox said. "Archuleta likes him, and Otero'll be back soon."

She went in without saying goodbye or wishing him a good trip. Ox went to his room long enough to get into his working clothes and pick up the Sharps rifle. The wagons were loading from the drays that had brought the goods from Welisch's warehouse, and Chucho Huerta was bustling around importantly, with Carlson laughing at him.

The seven-day round trip was easy—no bad grades and a good road. They pushed hard on the way to Florence, because of the perishable nature of the freight, but took it easy on the way back, with a load of pine planks transshipped from Prescott, for the brewery warehouse.

As they rolled down Main Street coming into Tucson, Ox was astounded to see Gwen coming through the traffic, waving at him. He hauled on the brake rope and yelled for Chucho. Chucho came running from the trail wagon. Ox jumped down, and Gwen grabbed his arm and said, "He's gone! Oh, Ben, he's gone!"

Traffic was piling up behind the wagons, and Ox turned to Chucho and said, "Can you take it on into the yard?"

"Sure, I take!" Chucho answered, and Ox let the brake off. Chucho mounted Lilly and popped the blacksnake. The mules knew they were only a few blocks from home, and started eagerly.

Gwen's face was white. She said, "Oh, Ben!"

Ox said, "Let's get inside," and took her arm.

In the book store, she said, "They held up the stage."

"Who?" he demanded. "What stage?"

Gwen said, "Flaco! The one he went on! And he's gone!"

Mansfield came out of the back room. "They dropped a horse to stop the coach and just shot them down," he said, "the driver and the guard and two passengers, a miner and a Mexican."

"Well, what about ... ?"

"He's just gone," Gwen said. "They didn't find a trace of him."

Mansfield said, "A teamster found them, couldn't have been half an hour later, because he remembers the two coaches passing him, the full one and that extra one. The marshal and that Pinkerton man left right away, and the deputy from Nogales met them. They found a trail, but it disappeared. They were down there three days."

Ox broke in: "Where was it?"

"A few miles this side of Calabasas."

Ox had a sickening memory of what he and Jake and Flaco had found not far from Calabasas—the flies and the stink and the six bodies—the little girl with the bloody skull and the hole in her back.

"I'll go down," Ox said. "First thing in the morning."

"There's no hurry," Mansfield said, "not after a week."

Ox hesitated, then asked what he didn't want to ask: "What about Lew and ... ?"

Gwen said, "Ben, you *couldn't* think that! You just *couldn't*!" But she didn't say they'd been in town last Saturday. And he and Ed Carlson had seen them ride out with a pack mule on Friday, set to stay out a while.

He said, "If they didn't find Flaco, maybe he got away. He could have jumped out and run into the rocks. He's probably with Archuleta right now." Gwen just stared at him, and Mansfield didn't say anything more, so Ox walked out and went to the livery.

Chucho had unhitched, and the wagons were standing there, still loaded. Carlson greeted Ox and said, "You can deliver the lumber to the brewery tomorrow. No hurry on it."

"Chucho can do it," Ox said. "I'm going down and see Archuleta."

"Well, I figured you would," Carlson said. "Can't get rid of the kid, can you! Send him away, and he's still makin' trouble for you."

"I have to, Ed," Ox said.

"Yeah, I know you do," Carlson said. "Well, let's go eat. You wanta wash up?"

After dinner, Ox found Benson in Foster and Hand's saloon. Benson couldn't tell him anything new. Two men had ambushed the stage and just cut loose and kept shooting until everyone was dead. Must have been drunk or crazy, with all the traffic on that road. The dead men were robbed, pockets turned out and watches gone. The first coach had the Wells Fargo box, so there wasn't any loss to the company, but maybe the two killers hadn't known that. Maybe they'd missed the first coach—maybe just got there to the road when the second one came along, and nothing else in sight for the moment, and figured all of a sudden they'd knock off all the witnesses and grab the box and run for the foothills of the Santa Ritas. Awful hard country. Couldn't track a horse far. He and Ogden and the Nogales deputy had spent three days looking.

"You got any idea it might have been Skin and Lew?" Ox asked, and Benson said, "Why not? They're still out of town."

"I'm going down to see Archuleta," Ox said.

"Who's that?"

When Ox had explained, Benson said, "Good idea."

Ox went home to bed.

By daylight, he was five miles out of town, with Lilly pounding along in that butt-breaking trot of hers. He was traveling light, with only a canteen, and a package of sandwiches and a few quarts of barley and a blanket wrapped in a slicker tied to the saddle strings. The Sharps, too long to carry in a saddle boot, was an awkward handful across his thighs.

They made the sixty miles in two days, and five miles out of Calabasas, Ox found the scene of the killing. There were a lot of mixed-up horse tracks and the skid marks of coach wheels. He found the hoof marks where two men had ridden away, overlaid by others that were probably from the mounts of Ogden and Benson and the deputy. He rode on, and turned into the track to Archuleta's place.

Archuleta saw him coming, and walked to the corral to greet him.

"Flaco didn't get here?" Ox asked, as they walked to the house.

Archuleta shouted for the fat woman to bring beer from the well. He sat in a rawhide chair at the rickety table, and said, "No, he's no come. I'm go to w'ere they shootin' that coach. Wass some wagon stop there. Men run aroun' in rocks, ever'body holler. Those four men dead. Flaco he's gone."

The smiling, fat woman brought two bottles of warm beer, and Archuleta twisted the caps off with his teeth and handed a bottle to Ox. He said, "I'm go along them horse track, two horse, where they goin' back into rocks, but pretty soon them track gone. Me, I'm not wanta follow them track an' get shot off my big nose. So I'm go home."

Ox tipped the bottle up and drank, and saw the three nails in a rafter, where the Apache scalps had hung.

"You wanta help me look for him?" he asked.

"Sure. I help. Tomorrow, eh? Pretty soon night. If he dead, he gonna stay dead."

They found Flaco late the next afternoon. Ravens and buzzards led them to the place, but it was Archuleta who led them to the buzzards. He wasted no time, but he didn't hurry. He missed no scraped rock, no hoof-cut twig, no overturned leaf that presented a bleached side to the sky. Most of the time, he seemed to follow the trail by intuition, because Ox couldn't see a thing. Finally, he rode up the bank of a wash and climbed a swell of hill, and gazed ahead as if he knew—and there were the circling buzzards.

The murderers had piled rocks on the boy. Ox turned away after the first, shocked glance. The long hair, the scalp bearing the scar from Lew's Colt, was gone. Archuleta said it was a very neat job. They piled on a few more rocks. Not that it would do any good—the coyotes had already been there.

Two nights later, Ox rode into Tucson. Only the night man was at the livery, and Ox rubbed Lilly down and put her in her stall.

He slept late and bathed and shaved off the week's whiskers, and had breakfast, then walked to the Pioneer News Depot.

When he walked in, she took one look at his face and knew what he had to tell. He said, "Gwen . . . I . . ." and she put her face in her hands. He walked around the counter and squatted on his heels by her chair and put his arm around her. She leaned her head on his shoulder. Mansfield came from the back room and stood looking at them. His eyes asked a question, and Ox nodded. Mansfield said, "Better take her home, Ox."

Gwen stood up and drew a long shuddering breath. She

said, "Poor little boy. He was so happy when he left." Mansfield brought her jacket.

They had almost reached Mansfield's house before she said, as though to herself, "I hate this place! I hate it!", and at the patio gate she said, "Thank you, Ben. You're the only one who cared anything about him. Everyone else wanted to kill him. And they did, didn't they? Even Lew hated him, didn't he?"

Well, Ox thought as he walked away, if she realized that, maybe it did some good. He went to the jail, and Benson and Owen Mason were there.

Ox sat down and said, "Well, I found him."

"Who?" Mason asked.

"Flaco. The kid. Up in the hills back of Calabasas. He was scalped. What are you going to do about it?"

"Nothin'," Mason said. "What's one Apache more or less?"

The marshal said, "Ox, we can't prove a damn thing. We'll get 'em dead to rights one of these days. Trouble is, you never know where they're gonna hit next. Now they're out of a job, they don't know what stage is carryin' valu'bles. They're li'ble to hit anywhere, just hit or miss. I think that's how come they hit that Nogales stage, when the money was in the first one."

"Who you talkin' about?" Mason asked belligerently. "You talk like you got the goods on somebody an' all you gotta do is bring 'em in."

"Don't be stupider'n you can help, Mason," the marshal said. "Every time they're out of town, somebody knocks over a stagecoach. Only, God damn it, how you gonna catch 'em? I'll lay you odds they won't be back in town again. They turned wolf, now."

"They're workin' a claim," Mason said. "What's illegal about that?"

"They bringin' in any samples for assay? You damn right they ain't. I'm gonna have a look at that claim."

"Good idea," Mason said, "if you knew where it's at."

"Won't be hard to find, 'less they're movin' camp every night."

"One thing," Ox said, "I could identify the kid's scalp, if they're the ones. It's got that scar where Lew slugged him with his gun. Supposing you could find it in their camp or some place. That'd prove they shot up the coach, wouldn't it?"

Benson said, "They prob'ly sold it to the Mexicans already,

along with them others, the ones you and Jake Harris found."

"Chris' sake!" Mason said, "You don't know it was them at all."

"I know it sure as I'm sittin' here," the marshal said. "You been a law man long as me, you'd know it, too. You get hunches."

"Hunches!" Mason snorted, and got up and went out.

"What about Lew's place?" Ox suggested. "Why don't we have a look. Might have left something around, stolen checks he couldn't cash or something."

"His place is padlocked," Benson said. "Judge Roberts told me I didn't have the evidence for a warrant, an' I can't just bust in on a hunch. But Barnes wouldn't be that careless. Nobody would."

Ox went to the livery office, and Carlson said, "You wanta go to Yuma for that steel for Etchells? He's in such a sweat for it, he stirred around and found us a load for Yuma, some of that lumber you brought down for the brewery. They don't need it all. He wrote to Kerens and Mitchell, an' they'll take it."

"It's a damn long haul, and hard on the mules," Ox said. "Take me a month."

"Well, it'll pay out," Carlson said. "That's what we got mules for, ain't it?"

chapter fifteen

It was sixteen days by freight wagon, more than 330 miles, to Yuma—sixty to Florence, then 273 more of stunning heat and dust devils and cactus and mirages—and history: the mysterious ruins of Casa Grande, Captain Moore's station at Maricopa, the ancient petroglyphs of Piedras Pintadas, Oatman Flats where Royse Oatman and his family were slaughtered by Apaches, the volcanic mass of Antelope Peak—only made bearable by frequent stage stations and teamsters' camps.

It was sixteen days of welcome bachelorhood for Chucho Huerta, and of worry for Ox. He was pretty sure Gwen's faith in Lew Barnes was deeply shaken, and that she probably shied away from admitting it to herself. She was stubborn and, like a mule when you pushed it to make it move over, was more likely to kick than to comply, and thus got itself into needless trouble. She might even go through with the marriage, out of sheer perversity and hurt pride, and sympathy for the underdog. And most likely she truly believed Lew to be no more than wayward and irresponsible. Ox could understand that, if she really loved him and was not just in desperate need of someone to cling to as a refuge from tragedy and sorrow, she could not believe him to be a rapacious monster. If you had friends, you were all the more loyal in the face of trouble.

So, when he swung the team into Yuma's single, wide avenue of hotels, restaurants, stores and saloons that led to Kerens and Mitchell's freight yard, he could hardly wait to exchange loads and start back.

He bought the Yuma Sentinel, and read it by firelight in their first camp on the return trip. There was no mention of any arrest of stage robbers and murderers of Mexicans, from which he concluded that Lew and Skin were still running loose. One item about Juan Pedro and his renegades closed with: The cavalry patrol and Indian Scouts, in relentless pursuit, have cut the renegades down to a mere half dozen. The savages raided the Wharton Ranch in the Aztec District on Wednesday last. Jay Wharton and his two sons escaped, but the murderers obtained fresh horses. This will only postpone their ultimate execution.

The last afternoon, coming into Tucson, Ox had to hold himself in check and not lay it into the mules, which were ga'nted up and weary, their hides muddied with a mixture of dust and sweat. When they unloaded the twenty tons of steel at Etchells' wagon factory, Ox felt as if twenty tons had been lifted off his back.

Carlson watched them come into the freight yard and said, "Come on in and cut the dust. Chucho can unhitch."

"He did more driving than me," Ox said. "Ask him in, too."

"Hell, he's a swamper," Carlson objected.

"No," Ox said, "he's a lot more than that."

"All right," Carlson said. "We'll give him a drink and a twenty-five dollar bonus."

"Fine," Ox said. "Hey, Chucho! Leave that! Let Pascual do it. All but Lilly. Give her a rubdown and put her in her stall."

Chucho got his drink and his bonus, and left for home, twice happy.

As Ox and Carlson went to Foster and Hand's saloon for the ritual before-dinner drinks, Lew Barnes and Skin Deschamps crossed Meyer Street a block ahead, riding toward Lew's place, with Skin leading the loaded pack mule behind his pinto.

Carlson and Ox stood at the bar with their drinks. Carlson said, "People are gettin' scared to ride the stages. Somebody took a whack at the Nogales stage again last week. Hit one of the lead horses, but didn't knock it down, an' the messenger sprayed the brush with buckshot an' they got away."

"I suppose they didn't recognize anybody," Ox said.

"Never saw anybody," Carlson replied. "They were forted up in the rocks."

"Are Lew and Skin working that claim?"

"That's the way they give it out," Carlson said. "They come into town every so often with a few ore samples."

"Well," Ox said, "either they've got all the gall in the world, or they're innocent."

Throughout dinner, there was no mention of Gwen, and Ox couldn't be sure Carlson wasn't avoiding the subject.

In the morning, he shaved off a month's whiskers and dressed in his best and, after breakfast, went to the Pioneer News Depot. He stopped short, outside the store. Lew Barnes was leaning on the counter and Gwen was looking up at him from her seat at the desk. Ox walked to the jail. Owen Mason was there with his feet on the desk. He greeted Ox with no enthusiasm, and presently Benson came in.

"You're back, huh?" he said, and Ox admitted he was.

Mason said, "Well, I'll take a *pasear* an' see who's in town. Gonna be hot again." He went out.

"I don't suppose you found out anything," Ox said.

"What's to find out?" Benson said. "One attack on a coach that didn't come off, while you was gone. Could've been anybody. But I tell you one thing, they lied about that holdup when Lew got shot. Ogden and me, we really went over the ground out there. Well, there wasn't no other horse tracks, just Tully's. They rode his horse around to mess up the tracks, but it was only the one horse, splay-footed nag that throwed its front feet sideways."

"So they *did* cut him down!" Ox said.

"Sure! They figured things was gettin' hot for 'em," Benson said, "so they bring in Tully dead. Proves they're innocent an' the other holdups was Tully's work, don't it? Who'd shoot his own partner?"

"What about that camp of theirs," Ox suggested. "Out on their claim?"

"Me an' Ogden been out there twice," Benson said. "They got a hole in the ground, all right, an' a windlass an' a singlejack an' a couple star drills, but they ain't workin' it, not really. Bring in a mule load of rock once in a while for assay, to make it look good, but that's all."

"What about the assays?" Ox asked. "Wouldn't that tell you whether they're hitting any color?"

"The assayer won't tell me nothin'," Benson said. "Says it's privileged. I'd get a court order, but I haven't got enough for the judge to listen to. An' now, I'm workin' alone. Ogden had to go to California on a train holdup."

In the morning, Mansfield was waiting for Ox in the patio of the hotel. He said, "Gwen wants you to take her to dinner. Wants to talk to you. Pick her up at the shop at six."

Ox's heart gave a great thump in his chest. "I'll be there," he said. "What about her and Lew?"

"I don't know," Mansfield said. "He keeps coming around. I don't know what she thinks. She won't talk to me. The son of a bitch is leaving this afternoon, going back to that so-called claim."

Mansfield left, and Ox passed the day somehow, killing time until six o'clock.

He took one of Carlson's rigs, a new, cut-under buggy pulled by a shiny chestnut gelding, and took Gwen to the Park Restaurant. He was glad to find the place nearly empty, and steered Gwen to a table in a corner.

They had fruit cocktail and salad, and suddenly Gwen reached across the table and took his hand. She said, "You and Lew used to be friends. What went wrong?"

"We never were close friends," Ox said. "It's just . . ."

She interrupted: "Do you really believe what everyone is saying? Do you?"

He said nothing, and she insisted, "Do you believe these things?", and waited for his answer.

"Gwen," he said, "it's not just me. Mansfield does, you know that. And the marshal and the Pinkerton man."

"I asked you what *you* think," she said.

"Maybe it is jealousy, partly," he said. "I've wondered myself. I guess you believe I love you. I do, Gwen. I can't say it right, but this is the first time for me, and it'll be the last. But I don't think I'd let that ... Gwen, you asked, and I'll tell you straight. He's no good. He'll bring you nothing but misery, even if he's innocent of those killings and holdups." He waited, expecting a tirade, but she only sat there still-faced and waited for him to go on.

"Maybe it's all coincidence," he said, "but he's been on the scene, or at least out of town, every time. *Every time*, Gwen! And I just can't see any man running with Skin Deschamps except by choice. Skin killed Jake, Gwen, and I'm not going to let it pass."

The waiter came with the roast and rolls and coffee, and they sat in painful silence until he had gone.

Ox went on: "In Ehrenberg, Lew asked me how much I thought you were worth. He quit his job to follow you. He's spent money he couldn't account for. Where does he get it?"

She was still silent.

"And what about Flaco, Gwen? It was Lew that hit Flaco with his gun . . ."

"Lew was drunk," she said. "He . . ."

"So was I," Ox said. "But drunk or sober, I wouldn't slug a fourteen-year-old kid with a gun."

She began to pick at her roast, and wouldn't look at him.

"Haven't *you* any doubts?" he asked. "Is this the kind of man you want to marry?"

"Yes," she whispered. He could hardly hear her. "Yes, I have doubts. I'm sick inside. You're the only one in the world I really trust." She got a handkerchief from her bag and patted her eyes. "I'm frightened. All the talk, all the hints. And he's changed, too. He's coarsened."

Ox watched her miserably. He said, "You don't want your dinner, do you? Shall I take you home?"

"All right," she said, but she didn't get up. "Ben, I can believe anything of Deschamps, those killings in the hold-ups, even that he killed my father. But how can I believe it of Lew? That he helped kill my father, and that he killed poor little Flaco? Ben, is he a thief and a liar? *Is* he a murderer?"

"Let's go home," Ox said.

She looked at the wadded handkerchief in her clenched

fist. "He keeps urging me to marry him right away. But I'm scared. I'm so scared that he . . ." She bit her lower lip and fought back tears.

Ox got up and held her jacket for her. He dropped money on the table and took her to the buggy. On the way home, he said, "One thing, Gwen . . . if they've really got a good thing going at that claim, it would go a long way toward showing they didn't need to hold up coaches for money. Have you seen any assay reports?"

"He says they're very good," Gwen said. "He . . . he wants me to lend him money to develop the claim."

"You haven't done it, have you?" Ox asked.

"I haven't got it yet," she said. "It's all settled, but I . . . well, I haven't sent for it."

When he escorted her through the patio to Mansfield's door, she said, "Thanks, Ben. I can't talk to anyone else. Those holdups and killings and scalping . . . I keep thinking he *couldn't!* But I don't know. *I don't know!*"

Her eyes looked scared, and he came near to grabbing her and babbling the love words that were whirling in his head—but she patted his arm and went in while he was trying to make up his mind whether he dared.

chapter sixteen

The run to Yuma had been hard on mule shoes, and harder on mules. When Ox told Carlson he was going to give the team a few days' rest, Carlson just said, "You're the mule man around here."

Chucho and Ox took the mules, four at a time, to the blacksmith shop and had them shod. The next day was taken up with minor repairs on the wagons and harness.

Carlson came out of the office about three, and walked over to where Ox was working. He said, "You hear about Zack Emory?"

"Who's he?" Ox asked.

"Foreman out at the Lizard Mine. Bob Leatherwood was

just in. Said somebody held up the mine office. Killed the bookkeeper an' shot Emory. They just brought him in to the hospital. You s'pose it was them *compadres* of yours, Lew an' Skin? You think maybe stagecoaches are gettin' too hot for 'em to handle?"

"By God, I *hope* it was them!" Ox said.

He went to the office and washed his hands in the big crockery bowl. Carlson watched him from the doorway. He said, "You gonna see that girl?"

"If it *was* Lew," Ox said, "she'll take it hard. I'd kind of like to be on hand."

"For her sake, or yours?" Carlson asked. "Maybe you're makin' a mistake, always thinkin' of her feelin's, handlin' her with kid gloves. Why'n't you just ask her straight out? If she'll have you, she will, an' if she won't, she won't."

When Ox came to the Pioneer News Depot, he saw Gwen at the desk, looking wavy through the window glass. Something about her, the slump of her shoulders, the air of dejection, stopped his greeting as he went in.

"Gwen," he said, "what is it?"

She looked at him apathetically, and said hello.

He walked around the counter and said again, "What is it?"

He heard Mansfield coming in from the back room, and turned to him. Mansfield said, "Ox, better leave her alone. Gwen, honey, why don't you go on home?"

Gwen said, "Thanks, John. I . . . I guess I will."

She refused to let Ox go with her. Mansfield got her jacket and held it for her and opened the door. He watched as she walked away, and said, "Rough on her right now, but she'll get over it. Best thing that ever happened."

"What?" Ox asked. "*What*, for God sake?"

"They got those two dead to rights," Mansfield said. "Held up the Lizard Mine office and killed the clerk and shot up Zack Emory, only they got careless. Zack's still alive, over in the Army hospital."

"*Who?*" Ox demanded.

"Lew and Skin Deschamps. Who else?"

"And he recognized 'em?" Ox asked.

"The stage had just delivered the payroll, and gone, and the shifts weren't due to change for an hour. Broad daylight, middle of the afternoon. A couple of quick shots, kill the only two witnesses, get into the brush fast with the payroll. Only it didn't work that way. They killed the clerk, and Zack took a slug in the back and one in the neck, but he crawled to the door and saw the two of 'em pulling out. They both had bandannas over their faces, but one of 'em had long hair and a beard. Rode a pinto, too."

"He recognize Lew?" Ox asked.

"No, but what's the difference?" Mansfield said. "They think they got away with it, most likely. Left Zack for dead. They'll come back into town, like after those stage holdups, and Benson'll sweat it out of 'em this time. Even if Zack doesn't make it."

"Didn't anybody go after 'em?" Ox asked.

"Sure. Whole gang of miners, getting in each other's way, messing up the trail. Nobody had a horse that could match the pinto and the other one."

"Well, what about Benson? Can't he . . . ?"

"He's been away three days, now," Mansfield said. "Him and Owen Mason and two Pima trackers."

Ox said, "She talked to me a little. She wasn't as sure about Lew as before. I . . . I guess this is hard on her."

"Tell you what," Mansfield said, "you come to dinner tonight. She needs friends, now, I guess."

"Sure," Ox said. "I'll go clean up. What time you want me?"

"Make it seven. That'll give me time to get home and tell Lucy. She'll want to polish the whole house."

Lucy Mansfield greeted Ox at the door. She said, "That awful Lew Barnes, I could . . . I could just . . ." It seemed she couldn't think of anything bad enough for Lew Barnes. She said, "Now, let's be gay, and cheer her up," and put on a bright smile and led Ox inside.

There was small talk in the living room for half an hour, and Mansfield brought out a bottle of brandy and served Ox and himself. Gwen smiled and missed questions and gave wrong answers, and everyone was relieved when Concha came in and said, "Come, ever'body! Deener raddy!"

Ox was wolf hungry and Concha a superlative cook. He applied himself, and joined in the small talk, and tried, as did the Mansfields, to include Gwen in it. No one spoke of what was on everyone's mind. Gwen waited listlessly until Ox had succumbed to Mrs. Mansfield's importunities and had a second piece of peach pie, then said, "Lucy, John, I'd like to talk to Ben by himself. Do you mind?"

Mrs. Mansfield patted Gwen's shoulder and said, "Of

course not, dear. John, we'll go for a walk, or sit in the patio or . . ."

"No, please," Gwen said. "We'll go out to the patio. Ben?"

Ox got up and said, "Best dinner I've had in Tucson, Mrs. Mansfield. Matter of fact, I'll say in Arizona." Gwen was already at the door, and he followed her into the high-walled patio. Dusk had fallen and stars were popping out. A nighthawk made a swooping dive across the last light in the west. Gwen led the way to a bench against the wall, and Ox sat beside her. He reached for her hand, but she pulled it away.

She said, "They don't know he did it. They don't *know* it was Lew."

Ox couldn't think of any reply.

"I . . . I guess it must have been Deschamps, all right," she went on. "With what Mr. Emory told them, the man that was shot. But it didn't *have* to be Lew with him, did it?"

Ox sat silent.

Gwen said, "Well?"

He said, "*I* can't prove anything, nor disprove it, either. What do you want me to say?"

"Nobody's ever gone to Lew's place and looked," she said. "All the talk, all the accusations. Why don't they go and see if there's any proof. They must put things *somewhere*, after they rob and kill."

"Who, Gwen? Who must?"

She looked away from him and caught her lower lip in her teeth. She said, "Deschamps and . . . and *Lew!*"

She was crying now, and he put his arm around her and pulled her close. She put her head on his shoulder, against his neck, the way she had that time he'd carried her to the shot-up, bloody coach that held her father's riddled body. He said, "Gwen, I can't believe either of 'em would leave anything around . . ."

"Yes, they would," she said. "Why wouldn't they? If nobody suspected them, they could just keep it there, the money or whatever it is."

"There's only one way to find out," Ox said. "Let's go and look. We won't find anything, but if it'll settle anything for you . . ."

"Thank you," she said. "I've got to know!"

Ox said. "We'll need a lantern. Want to walk around to the livery barn and I'll get one?"

She said, "I'll tell Lucy we'll be gone a while."

Half an hour later, as they walked along India Alegre through the alternate blots of shadow and splashes of soft lamplight from doorways and windows, Gwen said, "That's it in the next block, isn't it? I thought I saw a light inside."

Ox couldn't make out any light from the black shadow of the deep-set door and the one shuttered window. He stopped and lit the lantern he'd brought from the livery. In the stillness, he could hear scraps of conversation from nearby houses, and across the street, a horse stamped.

In front of Lew's shack, he set the lantern on the ground to one side, to leave room for him to back off and ram his shoulder into the flimsy door, and startled, saw the unlocked padlock hanging on the staple. Just then, Skin Deschamps yelled from the shadows of the alley across the street, "Lew!"

A body hurtled against the door from inside. The door slammed into Ox and knocked him off balance. As he went down, Gwen screamed and somebody leaped across him. Ox grabbed and caught a spurred boot, and he and Lew Barnes were all tangled up on the ground, thrashing around. Flat on his back, he swung his right fist and hit Lew somewhere, and Lew fought free and scrambled to his feet and ran.

There was a trample of hoofs, and Skin burst from the black mouth of the alley, his pinto dancing and trying to rear, and Lew's Morgan behind him, dragging at the reins with its neck stretched out.

Lew pulled his gun and fired back as he ran—a cracking shot and a flash of orange light—and Skin yelled, "Over here!"

Ox grabbed Gwen and threw her down. He clutched her to him and rolled with her and brought up against the adobe wall behind the setback of Lew's shack.

Gwen was moaning against his neck. He rolled clear of her and jerked his Colt from the holster and scrambled to the corner of the shack on hands and knees.

In the street, Lew was hopping with one foot in the stirrup, and the Morgan jerking back. Skin Deschamps spurred the pinto and yelled, "Come on, for Chris' sake!"

Ox waited until Lew swung into the saddle and made a silhouette. As he lined up on Lew, Gwen ran in front of him and shouted, "Lew! It's me! Gwen!"

Ox didn't dare fire, and Lew stopped the Morgan with a savage wrench on the reins. He swung it broadside and yelled, "You rotten, prying bitch!", and raised the gun and chopped it down.

Ox tackled Gwen as Lew fired. She screamed as he flung himself on her. Lew fired again, and the slug kicked dirt into Ox's face. He lay there sprawled on Gwen and heard the two horses pounding away.

He rolled off Gwen and got to his knees, but it was too late. Lew and Skin swung their horses into Meyer Street, heading south. People were cautiously putting their heads out of doorways and yelling questions, and a few came out onto the street.

Gwen got up and tripped over something and sprawled flat. Ox got her arm and hauled her up and, in the lantern light, saw what had tripped her. A dirty carpetbag lay there with one latch undone and money spilling out—bills and a few coins and some papers. Ox picked it up. People were gathering around plucking at Gwen and babbling questions as he picked up the lantern. Ox said, "Gwen, get inside!" and bulled his way, forcing a passage for her, through the increasing crowd. They went into Lew's shack, and three men tried to crowd in after them, but Ox shoved them back and pulled the door shut and set the lantern down.

Gwen's hair was in her eyes, her face was bruised and crusted with dirt. A lacy edge of camisole poked through a rip in her shirtwaist.

"Are you hurt?" Ox asked. "You weren't hit?"

"No. No. But ... oh, Ben!" The realization hit her now. She reached out to him, and he dropped the carpetbag and got his arms around her. She was crying—great wracking sobs. Suddenly she went rigid in his arms. He pulled his head back to look at her, and saw the horror in her eyes, and looked around to see what had shocked her so.

On the dirt floor was a bundle of scalps, perhaps a dozen. The one on top was Flaco's. He could see the long, puckered scar from Lew's gun. Gwen put her face against his chest and began to shake.

Owen Mason pulled the door open and came in. He turned and stuck his head out and said to those outside, "Keep the hell outa here!"

He swung around to Ox and Gwen and said, "What you doin' in here? You break that door open?"

Ox ignored him. Gwen collapsed against him, quiet now, and he said, "I'll take you home."

Mason grabbed Ox's shoulder and tried to pull him

around, and Ox slammed his elbow into Mason's ribs and turned, snarling. Mason backed up and said, "What's goin' on here? Who done the shootin'? God damn you, I'll . . ."

Ox growled, "Get out of the way!" and started for the door, pulling Gwen after him. His foot struck something, and he looked down and saw the dirt-encrusted carpetbag. He reached down for it, and told Owen, "Skin and Lew Barnes tried to kill her. Lew dropped this. You better get after 'em."

"Whaddaya mean, after 'em? You tell me what you're doin' in here!"

"You damn fool," Ox said, "this bag's full of money. And there's scalps. Flaco's scalp! They're the ones that shot up the Nogales stage and took him out and killed him. No other way they could have his scalp."

"Gimme that!" Mason said. "That's evidence." He reached for the carpetbag. Ox rammed him so hard with his shoulder that Mason slammed against the adobe wall, and dust came sifting down from the ceiling. "God sake, take it easy!" Mason said. He had a coughing fit before he got his breath back. He said, "That'll hang 'em, the bastards!"

"Bastards now, huh?" Ox said. "You've been jumpin' anybody that hinted they weren't Sunday school teachers."

"Well, nobody had no evidence," Mason said. He licked his lips, and his eyes wandered, not meeting Ox's scowl.

"Looks like they had it buried," Mason said, and motioned toward the corner of the room. There was a hole in the dirt floor, and a pile of dirt with a shovel stuck in it. "Let's see what's in it."

Gwen sat in the only chair and put her elbows on the table and her face in her hands. Ox turned the carpetbag upside down and shook it. Money fell out, loose bills and a few coins, and a few papers that looked like checks and Wells Fargo way bills. A gold watch and chain fell out last, and thumped onto the little heap of money.

"Yessir, this'll hang 'em," Mason said. He picked up the watch. "Stupid," he said. "Stupid to keep a thing like this."

Ox knew. He dropped the bag and moved to put himself between Gwen and Mason, but she had seen it.

She got up, not crying now, her face smudged and dirty and tear streaked. Ox tried to stop her, but she said, "Let me see it," and moved around him. She held her hand out and Mason gave her the watch and chain.

She studied it and gave it back to him. She turned to Ox and nodded her head. "Yes," she said, "it's his. It's Daddy's."

Mason said, "What? What's this? You reco'nize it? Miss, if you got any evidence, you tell me." He dropped the watch into the bag and began to put in the money and papers.

Ox got his arms around her shoulder and steered her toward the door, and Mason scuttled around in front of them and said, "Hold on, now! Just a minute, now!"

With his arm around Gwen, Ox went ahead as though he would walk right over Mason, and the deputy hastily pushed the door open and went out.

"Stand back there!" he ordered. "Let these people through!" He began to push people back.

"Don't forget who the watch belongs to," Ox said.

"Oh, no!" Gwen said. "I never want to see it again."

chapter seventeen

Someone was pounding on his door. Ox sat up in bed and rubbed his hands down his face, trying to come awake. "Who is it?" he demanded.

"Me. Mason."

Naked and sweating in the early heat, Ox got out of bed and walked across and unbolted the door. Mason came in. Ox sat on the bed and pulled the longjohns up his legs, and Mason said, "Jeez, you're sure put up! Like a Percheron or a Brahma bull."

Ox grunted something and Mason said, "Can you come over to the jail? Benson got in late last night. Wants to see you. He's been out tryin' to find them two, an' here they was right in town."

"All right," Ox said. "I'm going to eat first."

As they walked to the Maison Doree, Mason coughed nervously and said, "Well, I gotta admit I was wrong. Lotta rough characters around town. I can't ride a man just 'cause he's a hard case an' drinks an' blows off."

"Benson kept telling you," Ox said. "Couldn't dent your skull."

"Well, hell," Mason said, "there wasn't no real evidence till last night. Matter of fact, I could run you in for breakin' an' enterin'. It was that kid you brought home, there's the whole trouble, an' believe me, I got no use for 'Paches. You shouldn't've ... "

"What the hell did he have to do with them holding up stages?" Ox said. "Oh, hell, drop it!"

At the jail, Benson was red-eyed and bone-tired and old. He said, "Set down, Ox. God, I'm saddle galled! Never found no trace after they left the Lizard mine. Them army doctors don't give Zack Emory much chance, but we don't need him, after what you found in Barnes's place. Ties 'em to that Nogales stage holdup, an' the girl's father, both. Jury won't be out five minutes."

"We ain't caught 'em yet," Mason said. "They'll high-tail it. Maybe Mexico, huh? Pretty damn stupid, them hangin' onto all that stuff."

"Lew isn't famous for brains," Ox said. "Probably meant to sell the watch first chance. I bet Skin didn't know he kept it. I'd never've thought they'd risk keeping any of it here in town."

"Well," Benson said, "their best cover was to just keep comin' in to town, innocent like. Figured if they killed off the witnesses every time, nobody'd identify 'em. There's no doubt about the watch?"

"Gwen identified it," Ox said. "And there's Flaco's scalp."

"Owen," Benson said, "go get Miss Goodfield, will you? I gotta write out some statements."

"Leave her alone a few days," Ox said. "She was going to marry Lew. This is hard on her."

"Well, yeah, I guess so," Benson said. "Time enough when I bring them bastards in. Well, you tell me about it. I gotta get it in writin'."

"Aren't you wasting time?" Ox asked. "They'll be over the border in no time."

"I sent a lot of telegrams," Benson said. "There's posses out, an' Nogales got in touch with them Rurales across the line. They won't get clear. Anyway, they're broke, or they wouldn't've risked comin' into town. An' they didn't get what they come for. Prob'ly soon as they found out Emory didn't die, they knew they had to risk it for getaway money. An' if you an' the girl hadn't ... say, what was you doin' at Lew's place? You see them come in, or something?"

"We were there, that's all," Ox said. "What do you care why?"

"Guess I don't," Benson said. "Well, you start talkin' an' I'll write it down." He uncorked the ink bottle and got the pen in a death grip and began to chew his tongue, and Ox told him, a few words at a time. Benson kept saying, "Hold on, now. Not so fast," and it took an hour and a half.

When it was finished, Benson heaved a sigh and relaxed. He said, "You know, I don't figure we'll have to look far for them two. Figure they'll hit some more stages an' mines right around here, build them a stake before they head out. They can't travel the way they're gonna have to, without money. Can't ride the grub line, everybody'll be on the lookout for 'em."

Ox didn't see Gwen for three days. Something told him to stay away and not crowd his luck, if he had any. He dropped in at the Pioneer News Depot, and Mansfield told him she kept to her room most of the time, and hadn't said anything about Lew Barnes.

For once, Carlson didn't push Ox about finding freight to haul. He seemed to know Ox couldn't put his mind to business. Then, while Ox was having lunch in the Maison Doree, Mansfield came in and told him Gwen wanted to see him. Ox knocked his chair over and was picking up his hat when Mansfield said, "Now, don't go off like a rocket! She said about two o'clock."

Ox had time to go to his room and get shaved and polished up. When he went in through Mansfield's gate, she was in the patio. She looked pale, and didn't smile, but she held his hand when he sat beside her on the bench. She said, "I wanted to tell you I was wrong, and you were right all the time."

"You don't have to tell me anything," Ox said. "I didn't really know anything. I was half crazy with jealousy."

She wasn't wearing Lew's ring. She said, "I gave you a bad time, didn't I!"

"Not you," Ox said. "I gave myself the bad time. I knew you'd never look at me, Lew or not. But as long as you hadn't actually married him, I had to ... to keep on thinking maybe . . ."

She interrupted hastily, "Now that I know what he is, I'm not sure I really loved him. I *thought* I did. How do you know when you're in love? Whether it's just that you need someone?"

"You know it," Ox said. "Believe me, you know it!"

"Well," she said, "I want you to know it wasn't all so happy. He kept at me to get my money from Prescott, and he wanted me to go to bed with him. We were engaged, so it was all right, he said." She blushed, and looked away from him. "But I guess I liked the flattery, though, and all the thoughtful, generous things he did. But about you, Ben, from the very first you were my friend. Even when I was mad at you, I knew I could trust you."

He reached for her, but she pushed him away. They sat silent for a while, with Ox very conscious of her hand on his arm. At length, she said, "There's not a single thing that happened in Arizona, not one memory that doesn't hurt. The memory of Lew . . . I talk as if he's dead, don't I? . . . the memory of Lew is even worse than my father, because it was all lies and ugliness. And I knew you were right about him, after . . . well, after they killed Tully, but I kept lying to myself. I just couldn't let myself believe he was a beast of prey. How can innocent little boys grow up to be Skin Deschamps and Lew Barnes?"

"Lots of things, Gwen. Poverty and hardship, cruelties they've suffered, revenge for all the things they had to take and couldn't fight back. Lots of men had the humanity driven out of them by the war."

"You were in the war, too, Ben, and you're gentle and considerate. At least, when you haven't been drinking, and mad at somebody." He was embarrassed, thinking of the brawls she knew he'd been in. She said, "But you're never mean or cruel, and so far as I know, you never hit anybody that didn't need hitting."

"Gwen," he said, and his heart began to hammer like a stamp mill, "Gwen, after awhile, when you kind of get all this behind you, then maybe, well, could I . . . ?"

She looked at him gravely, and he couldn't go on. She said, "I've got to be by myself for a while. I have to think what I'm going to do, where I'm going to be."

"Aren't you going to be here?" he asked.

"I think California," she said. "Not Arizona, not ever again."

Before he could think of a protest, she went on, "I'll stay a while. Mr. Mansfield's going to expand the business, and he's been so good to me and I know his books and all the business, now. I won't go till he has things running smoothly."

"Well," he said, "can I see you? I'll be around, and . . ."

"Not for a while, Ben. I want to think things out all by myself. I'll go to Prescott and get that business settled, then,

I think Santa Barbara. Have you ever been there? A nice, quiet town and a long, curving beach, and no heat and no winter. And nobody carries a gun."

"Sounds good," he said. "They haul freight over there, too, don't they?"

She laughed. "Yes, they do! The most beautiful mules I ever saw. You'd be in seventh heaven."

Ox went back to work. He and Chucho took a load to Nogales, and spent a day and a night with Archuleta and got a little drunk on his warm beer.

When they got back, Ox went to the jail to see if Lew and Skin had been run to earth. Owen Mason said Benson was out hunting them. None of the posses had found anything and no one had reported seeing them.

Gwen was busy again at Mansfield's office work, while Mansfield superintended the building of the addition. Ox walked her home nights and took her to dinner when she would go, and avoided mentioning what was in his heart, because she obviously wanted it that way.

He made two trips to Florence, and one to Phoenix, and a month went by. There was one more robbery of a mine office, and one more dead man. A Mexican sheep herder said Lew and Skin had stayed two days at his camp, and a posse found their trail and lost it.

Then they held up a stage at the same old place, Point of Mountain, not twenty miles out of Tucson. They didn't kill anyone, and seemingly didn't care that they were recognized. Owen Mason said that now they were out in the open, so to speak, they knew every holdup would be laid at their door, anyway, so there was no need to eliminate witnesses. This time they had downed a horse, as usual, but had sat back in the rocks, not risking an approach to rob the passengers, and ordered the driver to throw the box down and cut the dead horse clear, and move on.

They kept on the move; their camps were found, just ashes in a fire pit, sometimes still warm, and never less than twenty miles from the last night's camp. They made an attempt to get across into Sonora, but the Rurales almost caught them, and ran them ten miles back into Arizona before they lost them. Mine offices were guarded night and day, and temporary deputies rode the stages.

Deputy Marshal Benson came back for a rest, half-dead

on his feet. He said they were gradually closing in on the two, encircling them, driving them into a smaller and smaller compass, and that it was just a matter of time. A sheepman was found shot, apparently for nothing more than the food in his camp. Benson said the proceeds of the last stage holdup weren't any good to Lew and Skin because they didn't dare appear any place where they could buy supplies. They must be damn hungry and desperate. If somebody didn't put a slug through them, they'd likely make a try at breaking through the encirclement, whether they built up a stake or not. They'd changed horses a half dozen times, stealing fresh ones when they needed them, and riding them to death in their desperate game of hide-and-seek. Their great handicap was the country. Nobody could just point a horse in the chosen direction and go—it was too steep and broken and rough, and there wasn't enough water.

Tucson was full of false reports, and everyone knew how the pursuit should be handled. The "Arizona Daily Star" was sarcastic in its editorials, criticizing U.S. Deputy Marshal Benson and the army, from the Secretary of War down to Sergeant Finlay. Volunteer heroes began to quit the posses. And still, Lew Barnes and Skin Deschamps weren't caught. For several weeks, there were no attempts at hold-ups. Undoubtedly they knew of the extra guards and the alertness of passengers. Only a frontiersman of Skin's experience could have dodged capture this long, considering the impossibility of traveling the mountains except by known trails and water holes. The "Daily Star" turned on the invective when a patrol killed one of Juan Pedro's desperate Apaches, but let the other half dozen sift through its fingers. It began to look as if the Apaches had got themselves caught in the net spread for Barnes and Deschamps, or vice versa.

Ox and Chucho returned from a short haul to Camp Lowell. Before they left, Ox had arranged to take Gwen to dinner the night he got back. He called for her at the Pioneer News Depot, and Mansfield proudly showed him the new addition. Ox's elation at the prospect of an evening with Gwen evaporated. She had said she'd stay only until Mansfield's addition was completed and the business operating smoothly again.

He took her to the Park Restaurant in one of Carlson's buggies. Once seated and dinner served, he was afraid to ask when she planned to leave. She brought it up, herself: "I'm going to Prescott next week and arrange to transfer my

money to Santa Barbara. I'll be so glad to get out of
Arizona." There was a tightness in his chest and he couldn't
think of anything to say.

"I won't pretend, Ben. I won't ask if you're going to miss
me. I'll miss you, very, very much. You and John and Lucy."

He found his voice. "How about me coming to California,
too?"

"You've got a fine start in business, Ben. You can't just
walk away from it."

"What's to stop me?" he asked. "I've got some money piled
up. I don't know how much, but enough for a team and
wagons."

"Ben, don't you see? You mustn't rush me, it's too soon!
Too soon after . . ."

"I meant," he interrupted hastily, "we could be married
here, and then go to California." He stopped and looked
away, then rushed on, with the words tumbling out, "Room
in a wagon for trunks and gear and a water barrel, and we
could take our time, maybe a month or two to get there, see
the country. Away from everybody, and you could kind of
forget about things."

Well, he'd said it, and was deeply afraid of her answer, but
immensely relieved to have got it out.

"I honestly don't know how I feel about you," she said.
"It's too soon. And what I'm afraid of . . . Ben, I'm afraid
every time I saw you I'd be reminded of what happened to
Daddy and all the awful things with Lew. Because, don't you
see, you were a part of all of it. Ben, please don't, not yet."

Ox said, "All right, Gwen. But let me do one thing. With
those two not caught, nobody's safe traveling. Those Apaches
are somewhere around, too. I don't want to scare you, but
Skin and Lew have a habit of just pouring lead into a coach,
regardless. I'll borrow Carlson's Dougherty wagon and take
you to Prescott, so I'll know you're safe."

She thought about it while he waited anxiously. "I *am*
afraid of riding the stage and, Ben, I'm deathly afraid of
Lew. I know he wasn't just shooting that night to stop you
from coming after him, he was trying to kill me. Why does
he hate *me*?"

"I think it's your money, Gwen. He thought he had it in
his hands. And then, of course, it was you and me that found
the loot that night, and Flaco's scalp . . . the evidence that
really proved everything."

She hadn't said yes or no about his taking her to Prescott.

He said, "Gwen, listen. There's good stage stops for every night. With six good mules and that light wagon, we'd stop early each day. We'd be in Florence the second night, and Phoenix the next. Then . . ."

"Well, if you really want to, Ben."

"That way, I'll know you're safe," he said.

Then she spoiled it. She said, "But if you're concerned for me, why couldn't you just go with me on the stage?"

He was going to emphasize the murderous habits of Lew and Skin, and remind her of the Apaches, but it was pretty lame—actually, she would be as safe on the stage. He fumbled for an answer, when she laughed and said, "I'm just deviling you. I want to go with you, and I'll feel safer, too. But it will be a great scandal, won't it!"

He grinned, sweating with relief. "We'll take Chucho," he said. "Two pairs of eyes and two guns till we get out of the danger area."

He took her home, and didn't let his thoughts roam past next week when she'd be gone, just kept thinking of the trip.

In the morning, when Carlson arrived at the livery, Ox was already there looking over the Dougherty wagon, in the wagon shed. The Dougherty, a high-wheeled, rugged vehicle with springs at the corners and three upholstered seats and a boot for luggage, was usually pulled by four mules—at least, that's the way the army did it—but Ox decided he'd use six, and drive with a jerk line. His mules weren't used to reins. He figured he could sit with Gwen instead of riding Lilly, and drive from the front seat.

"You gonna branch out into the livery business?" Carlson asked. "Like to sell you that Dougherty. It don't get hired out once a month, too heavy for runnin' around town."

Ox said, "I'm only going to borrow it, and six mules. I've got a passenger for Prescott, Friday."

"Just a spin up to Prescott an' back, huh?" Carlson said. "Two weeks or better with six of our mules. So what am I gonna haul freight with? An' who's gonna drive for me?"

Ox felt like a fool. "Ed, I just wasn't thinking. I was even going to borrow Chucho. Gwen's going to California and not coming back. I have to go, Ed. I'm going to see her safe as far as Prescott. Lew and Skin and those Apaches aren't operating that far."

"Not comin' back?" Carlson said. "You go ahead, boy. Take the damn wagon. Take Chucho, too."

"By God, Ed, you're a . . ."

"Aw, forget it," Carlson said. "I'll have a couple of the boys roll it out an' grease it."

chapter eighteen

Ox went to the Pioneer News Depot. Gwen was, to Ox, more beautiful than ever. He had been hoping she might have changed her mind about leaving, but there was no sign that she had any regrets. She was subdued, and talked about last minute things she had to do, and said he was to come to Mansfield's for dinner.

He had a premonitory wrench of loneliness, and put it out of his mind, determined not to think about anything but being alone with her (Chucho didn't count) for six days. Time enough after that to start living with the emptiness.

He spent most of the day checking the wagon and loading the emergency items no desert traveler left behind—a couple of canteens, a keg of water, a sack of barley for the team, blankets and a tarp. He wouldn't be riding Lilly, so he put her saddle in the boot.

Chucho was eager to go, and understood his role, which was to keep the Winchester carbine cocked in his hands, and to look behind every rock and saguaro and clump of creosote, and up every draw and sidehill, and to yell at Ox if he even suspected anything was moving.

Dinner at Mansfield's was not a happy occasion. Gwen and Mrs. Mansfield were on the verge of tears and Mansfield was morose.

Gwen had a big trunk and two suitcases and a carpetbag packed and waiting in the hall. She said an absentminded "goodnight" to Ox, and she and Lucy Mansfield dabbed at their eyes with handkerchiefs.

Mansfield went out to the patio with Ox. He said, "I'm not too pleased about this. She'd be safer with other passengers and a guard on the stage."

"John," Ox said, "when Lew and Skin hit a stage, they just pour the lead in without warning. Nobody knows where they'll show up. There's nothing about a wagon to tempt them. I won't trust her to anyone else."

Chucho had the six mules hitched when Ox got to the livery stable in the morning. They went to the Maison Doree for breakfast, and drove to Mansfield's about nine. Ox was lavish with the whip on the way to Mansfield's, to work some of the cussedness out of the team before Gwen got aboard.

Gwen kissed Mansfield's cheek before she and Lucy Mansfield fell weeping into each other's arms. Lucy blubbered and said, "I know you'll take care of our girl," and fled into the house.

Ox and Chucho loaded the luggage into the boot and Chucho took his place on the rear seat, where he could have a clear view both sides. Mansfield hugged Gwen and kissed her before he boosted her over the wheel.

Rested and full of go, the six mules hit their collars with a rush when Ox hollered and laid on the whip. He yelled, "Gee!" and they swung into Stone Avenue with Gwen gazing back through her tears until Esteban Ochoa's house cut Mansfield's from view.

Outside the town, with the mules pounding along at a gallop, Ox passed a freight rig and swung in behind the Florence stagecoach. He decided to stay with the coach as close as he could so they could reinforce each other in case of trouble. There wasn't much chance to do so, because the coaches traveled the fifteen or twenty miles between stations and a change of horses at a headlong gallop.

The traffic thinned out and the coach gradually pulled ahead. Ox gave up trying to keep it in sight and let the mules settle into a trot. They were going forty miles that day, and couldn't do it at a run. The morning was brisk and beautiful, and the sun was beginning to strike through the canvas top. Gwen took her jacket off and pushed her hand under Ox's arm. Over the creaks and rattles and the steady pound of hoofs, they could hear Chucho singing off key, some heartbroken Mexican song about the treachery of a faithless lover.

They slowed for the first grades where the road began to wind into the foothills of the Santa Catalinas. With three hours behind them, Point of Mountain was only a few miles ahead, and Ox worried a little, because two of Lew and Skin's holdups had been pulled along this stretch and this was where they had shot Tully down. Ox could picture the shock of sudden realization on Tully's ugly face when Skin turned the shotgun on him—the desperate grab for his Colt, the frantic shot that caught Lew Barnes in the arm, the gasping death in the dust. Too bad Tully hadn't hit Lew six inches to the right. Would have saved a lot of misery for everyone.

The shot echoed off the hills, and Tom, the nigh leader, screamed and reared and fell across Jerry.

For one stark second of shock, Ox and Gwen and Chucho sat rigid while the wagon swung and skidded and the mules went crazy, plunging and tangling themselves in the traces.

The wagon slid sideways to a stop. Dust swirled, and over the racket of the frantic mules, there was another shot. Tom was on the ground now, dead. Ox pushed Gwen out. She fell and got up, and he jumped down and dragged her behind the dead mule. The rest of the team, kicking and bucking, were jerking the body. Ox lay on Gwen and, with shod heels flashing past his head, managed to unhook the two traces. The five mules, in a snarl of chain and harness lunged and stumbled and moved to one side.

In the dust cloud, Ox yelled in Gwen's ear, "Stay down!" and ran to the wagon and got the Sharps and the cartridge belt. As he bent over and ran back, shots began to blast out on the side of the wagon away from the hill. Ox threw himself down and twisted over, cursing, and saw Chucho Huerta prone between two rocks, pouring shots at random up the hill.

Ox clawed his way with his elbows, with the Sharps across his forearms, and lay flat beside Gwen. The firing stopped. Chucho had shot the carbine empty and was reloading. At least, he had kept somebody's head down while Ox got the Sharps.

The mules, hopelessly entangled, quieted down. Over Tom's body, Ox stared along the barrel of the heavy rifle and saw nothing but rock and saguaros and cholla on the hillside. Chucho began to fire again, and Ox yelled, "Chucho! Save it!"

A rifle fired from the hill, and the slug screamed off one of Chucho's rocks. Chucho fired again, and Ox shouted, "Chucho! Cut it out! Wait till you see something!"

Up the hill, somebody called out, "We got a bonus, Lew! It's her an' that mule-skinnin' son of a bitch!" The voice was Skin Deschamps'.

"Lew!" Ox yelled. "We've got nothing! A few dollars!"

Lew Barnes laughed. Chucho fired twice, and Skin De-schamps shot back, another ricochet that whined and faded away.

Barnes yelled, "You got mules, and that's what we came for. Horses can't stand the gaff."

"You can have 'em!" Ox answered.

"God, you're generous!" Lew yelled. "We'll take the mules and the bitch, too! And leave you for the buzzards!"

Ox stared till his eyes watered, searching behind every rock and bush for a cast shadow that might show the shape of a man. He saw nothing but the rocks and cactus.

Gwen mumbled something and moved, and Ox pushed her flat with his elbow and said harshly, "Keep down!" He looked both ways, up and down the road, hoping, hoping ... There was nothing, no freight wagons, no coach ...

Chucho fired again, and Skin Deschamps swore. Ox stared toward where Skin's voice had sounded, and suddenly saw him! Just a piece of a hat, and a hand sliding a carbine across a rock.

Ox took his time. He wiped sweat from his eyes and got two cartridges from the belt and laid them on the ground. A little more of Skin showed, more shoulder and arm, and a brown hand with three fingers around the stock and a forefinger on the trigger, not fifty yards up the hill. He wasn't trying for Ox—seemed to be angling for a better shot at Chucho. Ox lined up the sights and began to squeeze his right hand together.

Lew fired. Ox jerked and swore and managed not to fire. Out of the tail of his eye, he saw the smoke roll out from behind Lew's rocks.

Skin's shoulder still showed. Ox fired—a blast of sound, a ball of white smoke—and a shriek from Skin.

Through the dispersing smoke, he saw Skin stand erect and pitch down over the rock, rolling over and over in a small landslide of dirt and gravel. Ox slammed the lever forward, jammed a cartridge into the breech, swung the lever shut and shot him again as he rolled. The body caught behind a prickly pear and lay crumpled.

Ox threw the lever forward and groped for the other cartridge on the ground. Gwen moaned and grabbed his arm, and he dropped it.

Chucho shouted, "Ox!"

Lew Barnes was running up the hill, tripping, grabbing cactus branches, heedless of thorns, hauling himself along. Ox snatched up the cartridge belt and pulled another cartridge out. He shoved it into the fuming breech and jerked the lever home.

Lew broke into an open stretch of arroyo and dove behind a tangle of brush. Ox rose to his knees and swung the Sharps into line. Gwen clung to his arm, crying. He swore at her and knocked her away with his elbow.

Lew plunged into view on a small horse, with his right foot out of the stirrup driving in the spur. Ox swung the Sharps too late. Lew disappeared among the rocks.

"Chucho!" Ox yelled. "Why didn't you nail him?"

"I'm empty! I'm loadin'!" Chucho shouted back.

For a few minutes they could hear stones sliding and hoofs striking rock as Lew spurred up the arroyo.

Ox leaned the Sharps on the dead mule and stood up, and Gwen threw herself on him and clung to him, sobbing. He held her, looking down on the bright hair with the dirt ground into it, patting her shoulder and telling her to hush.

Chucho walked over from his rock fort and said, "Jeez, I wass scare'! I cou'n't get them shells in that li'l hole in side of gun."

"You did fine," Ox said. "You got it loaded now?"

"Sí, she got bullets," Chucho said. Sweat and dust made a brown paste on his face and his sleeve was torn, showing a scrape on his arm from his dive behind the rocks.

Gwen shuddered and stopped crying, but kept her face pushed into Ox's chest and mumbled, "Are they dead?"

"Skin is," Ox said, "and Lew will be when I catch up with him."

She wiped her nose on her sleeve and made motions at her hair, which was a tangle down her back. Ox steered her gently to the wagon. The mules jumped when they came close and Ox yelled curses at them and Gwen started crying again. He helped her to climb in, and she sat hugging herself, with tears making bright tracks through the dirt on her face.

It took Ox and Chucho fifteen minutes of coaxing and swearing and dodging kicks and untangling spreaders before the mules were straightened out. Ox unharnessed Lilly and saddled her and hung both canteens on the saddle horn.

Gwen said, "Where are you going?"

"After Lew," Ox said.

"He got big head start," Chucho said.

"He won't get far. He's got no sense about a horse. Lilly will run him down."

"Are you going to kill him?" Gwen asked.

"You think he should be left running loose?" Ox asked. When she didn't answer, he said, "You'd rather see him hang?" He turned to Chucho. "Take her on to Point of Mountain. First wagon or coach you meet, send me some help."

"Sure, I do that," Chucho sidled up to Cactus and put his hand out slowly and caught the bit ring. Cactus walled his eyes and reared, and Chucho talked to the big wheeler and calmed him.

Gwen said, "I want to go home."

Ox thought it over a moment and said, "Well, I guess it's all right. Go on back to Tucson, Chucho. Take her to Mansfield's, then find Benson or Owen Mason. They'll get up a posse. And lay it into those mules. Make 'em move."

Ox got up on Lilly, with the Sharps across the saddle fork. She balked, and he kicked her with both heels. She plunged ahead and went into a trot and, as he headed her up the arroyo, Gwen called, "Ben!"

He stopped Lilly and looked back. She said, "Let him go! Don't go!", and the bitter thought came to him that she still loved Lew, in spite of everything.

"I'll bring him back to you, if that's what you want," he said. "I'll dump him right in your lap. With his guts shot out."

"*Oh, no!*" she wailed, and began to climb down over the wheel. "Ben! Wait!"

He slacked the rein and kicked Lilly into a trot.

"I don't mean *that!*" she cried, stumbling along after him. "It's *you!* I'm afraid for *you!*"

He kicked Lilly again, and she began to pick her way carefully upward among the rocks and cactus.

There was no tracking to do. Lew had been trying to cover ground, nothing else, and the marks were plain—displaced stones and places where the horse had slipped. Ox let Lilly set her own pace, and looked ahead warily, trying to anticipate an ambush, listening to the stillness. Lilly plugged along conserving her strength with mule wisdom, stopping occasionally to rest, then going on of her own accord.

He guessed it was about two o'clock when he found Lew's

horse dead, just a rack of bones slashed by spurs, used up even before the heartless drive up the arroyo. Lew had simply ridden it to death.

Ox rode half a mile farther along Lew's footprints, then began to get scared, and tied Lilly in the shade of an overhanging cliff. He loosened the cinch, and gave her a drink from his hat, and took a sparing drink himself. He slung the other canteen, the full one, over his shoulder and went on, with the cartridge belt around his waist and the big rifle in his hand.

Wherever the broken ground leveled out, Lew had run, and Ox knew he couldn't keep that up very long. He went now with exaggerated caution, stopping for minutes to peer around boulders, studying each branching colony of prickly pear, going wide around open places, keeping in the brush and against the hot rock walls. His shirt stuck to his back, and he had to keep wiping sweat from his eyes.

Lew fired too soon. Ox threw himself sideways and rolled behind rocks and a screen of creosote bush.

Lew called, "Ox! Is that you? Listen! Go on back!" So Lew hadn't seen him yet, had only heard him coming and hadn't had sense enough to hold his fire. "I'll let you go!" Lew yelled. His voice bounced back and forth in the canyon.

Ox picked up a piece of rock and tossed it to one side. Instantly Lew fired. The oldest trick in the book, one Ox had read in some dime novel when he was a kid, and Lew fell for it! And now Ox knew where he was. The mottled shadows of mesquite branches made it as hard as trying to spot a rattler in fallen leaves, but Ox stared under the wispy layer of smoke that hung still on the hot air, and the outline began to appear. At first he thought it was Lew's head. Then he recognized the round object as a canteen.

He aimed carefully and fired. The canteen jumped and rolled down toward him, spouting water from both sides.

Lew squawked and leaped up, and dropped back out of sight as the echoes rolled.

Ox called, "Get set for a long stay, Lew. I've got water."

Lew fired at Ox's voice, and came close. Ox ground his face into the dirt, and heard Lew work the lever of his carbine.

Another rifle blasted, not forty yards to one side. Lew yelled and stood up behind his rock and fired two rapid shots. An Apache hurtled out of the rocks, bent low, running toward Lew, and two more leaped onto his back and bore him down.

Ox ran.

He ran as hard as he could go down the arroyo, caroming off rocks and tearing his way through cactus. Two shots followed him and whined off the rocks. He fell and rolled, and got up, and threw the canteen away as he ran.

Behind him, he heard the first scream, Lew's gargling shriek of agony. Ox kept on running—giant, plunging steps down rock slides and gravel fans until he was staggering and fighting for breath. He sat on a rock, streaming sweat, until his chest quit heaving, then got on hands and knees and crawled behind a heap of broken rock that had fallen from an overhang.

How the hell had those Apaches been right there, at that precise moment in time and space! They had to be Juan Pedro's bunch, most likely caught in the circle of army patrols and Indian Scouts that had been converging on Lew and Skin—maybe even trailing Lew and Skin, themselves, and drawn by the sounds of the battle down at the road.

Ox heard someone coming. Lew howled again, an animal sound like nothing human. An Apache flitted across an open place up the arroyo, and was gone. Ox stared up the arroyo, past a shoulder of vertical rock where anyone coming down would have to pass. He slid the Sharps out between two rocks. As far as he could tell, only one Apache had passed the shoulder of rock.

Juan Pedro sprang up howling, thirty yards away, and ran straight at him, brandishing a carbine. Ox fired. The 475-grain bullet took Juan Pedro in the breast bone and flung him backward over a rock. His feet hung down, drumming a moment on the rock, and were still. The soles of his moccasins were worn through.

Up the canyon, Lew's voice came low and querulous, like the mewing of a kitten. For a moment, Ox didn't recognize it as the sound of the last extreme of agony.

He reloaded and went slowly down, still taking advantage of cover and walking crouched, staggering with exhaustion and blundering into rocks, with his face over his shoulder. He saw nothing and heard no pursuit, and at last came to Lilly. He tightened the cinch and got on, and let her set her own pace, picking her way down to the road.

He kept looking back, with his back muscles cringing, expecting the shock of an Apache bullet. When Lilly braced her legs and stopped, he wasn't expecting it, and almost went over her head. She had her nostrils flared and her ears pointing ahead past a jumble of rocks. How could anyone have got ahead of him? If they'd followed him, they'd have shot him before now. But maybe—and the thought shocked him—maybe some of the band had been down by the road all the time! And if they had, what if Chucho hadn't got away fast enough?

In the silence, he heard a click, the hammer of a gun being cocked. He threw himself out of the saddle and rolled behind a rock, and waited, sweating, but cold inside. Nothing happened. Nothing moved. He laid the Sharps down and drew the Colt and cocked it, and began to crawl across the canyon, ignoring the thorns and the scraping of knees and elbows on the harsh ground.

He crawled for twenty minutes, between pauses to listen, and went about forty feet before he slowly took off his hat and raised his head to stare behind the jumble of rocks.

Gwen was crouched there, with Chucho's carbine pointing up the canyon.

He said, "Gwen!" and stood up.

Gwen screamed and dropped the carbine, and covered her face with her hands.

Ox ran to her, crashing through the cactus and brush. He knelt and gathered her in his arms, and she clung to him and put her face in the hollow of his neck.

"It might have been *him*!" she said. "It *could* have been!"

"Where's Chucho?" Ox asked.

"He's back with the wagon."

"I'll kill him!" Ox said.

"No, Ben! I wouldn't leave, wouldn't go back to Tucson, and he was going to go after you. But I couldn't stay there waiting and not knowing." She was crying, and he could hardly understand her. "I snatched the gun from him and started after you, and he ran after me, but I told him he had to stay and stop the first coach or anything that came along the road, and send help. You mustn't blame him. I made him do it."

She shuddered and clung tighter. "And I heard the shots and I kept trying to run, and falling down, and I didn't know if it was you or ... or ... whether it was you or Lew coming down, when I heard the horse. I didn't know if it was Lew."

"He's dead," Ox said. "He'd have killed you, don't you know that?"

"No," she said. "I'd have killed *him*! Even if I knew you were dead, I'd have killed him."

"We have to go," Ox said. "There's Apaches up there."

He heard the scrape of hard soles on rock, below in the canyon, and Chucho's voice saying, "Here her track. Hurry up!"

Ox set Gwen on her feet. Chucho and five men came around an outthrust of rock. Chucho saw him and tried to run, with his boot soles slipping on the gravel. "You awright?" he shouted. "You not hurt? Ox, I coul'n't help it! She make me stay. An' I stop stage coach, an' these feller . . ."

"Where's Barnes?" one of the men asked. He had a carbine. One of them had a shotgun, and the other three had Colts in their hands.

"He's dead," Ox said. "And you better watch it. There's Apaches up there. I killed Juan Pedro, but there's some of his bunch . . . "

"We'll flush 'em out, 'less they got away."

"Le's go," one of them said. "You better get her down to the road. Send us all the help you can scrape up, will you?"

"There's a telegrapher at Point of Mountain," Ox said. "I'll get on the wire to Tucson."

Gwen clung to Ox as the five men scrambled on up the canyon. When they went around a bend, Ox said, "Chucho, Lilly's up there a ways. Bring her down, will you?"

"Sure," Chucho said.

While they waited, Ox said, "We'll go to point of Mountain and get you to bed. I'll send a wire to Tucson, and one to Mansfields so they'll know you're all right. We can head out for Prescott in the morning."

She kissed him, then, and left no doubt that she meant it. She said, "I'll go to Prescott with you, or back to Tucson, or anywhere in the world with you. But not anywhere without you, not ever again."

She meant that, too.

Ox thought his heart might hammer a hole in his chest. He pulled her close, hugging so tight she gasped for breath. She whispered, "Closer, Ox! Closer!"

Chucho led Lilly down and stopped beside them. He said, "You know what gonna happen, don't you? Kids! Whole lot of kids. You gonna be damn sorry, like me."

Gwen grinned at him. She said, "Twenty? In pairs, like a team of mules? I'd like that."